CW00507087

THE COFFEE BREAK COLLECTION

SHORT STORIES, FLASH FICTION & POETRY

BY

THE WORDSMITHS

THE COFFEE BREAK COLLECTION

SHORT STORIES, FLASH FICTION & POETRY

By

The Wordsmiths

Paperback edition

Grateful thanks to Rob Tysall, Tysall's Photography for the cover imagery.

ISBN: 9781696547994

CONTENT

Title	Author	Page
The Shadow	Marilyn Pemberton	9
Shadows	Mark Howland	11
Shadow	Mary Ogilvie	14
Passion	Mary Ogilvie	14
Smile	Mary Ogilvie	14
The Knock	Ann Evans	15
My Time	Margaret Mather	19
Erasing History	Catherine Wilson	21
Poetic Excuse	Bec Woods	24
Quotations	Mary Ogilvie	25
Alphabetti	Maxine Burns	26
Alphabetical Poem	Marilyn Pemberton	27
What's in a Name	Alex Bartlett	28
Arctic's Night	Mark Howland	29
A Kind of Magic	Mark Howland	29
Beauty Spot	Margaret Mather	30
Music Never Stops	Ella Cook	32
Mam	Maxine Burns	34
Dad	Maxine Burns	36
Pancho	Catherine Wilson	39
The Blue Bench	Margaret Mather	41
Comrades	Jackie Skipp	45
Going to Hurt	Alex Bartlett	46
Live – Here!	Robert Tysall	47
The Piano	Marilyn Pemberton	49
Night of Hell	Alex Bartlett	51
Dead End	Marilyn Pemberton	53
Rain or Shine	Robert Tysall	57
Star Source	Alex Bartlett	59
About a Cat	Catherine Wilson	60
The Hunt	Maxine Burns	61
The Dungeon	Marilyn Pemberton	63
Two of a Kind	Mary Ogilvie	64
A Very Special Gift	Ann Evans	71
One Silent Night	Maxine Burns	81
Convenience Store	Bec Woods	86
Out with the Old	Marilyn Pemberton	90
Retail Therapy	Bec Woods	91
The Kingfisher	Catherine Wilson	96

Title	Author	Page
Business or Pleasure, Miss?	Alex Bartlett	98
Beware Innocent Looking	Ella Cook	100
Waiting	Marilyn Pemberton	103
Food	Marilyn Pemberton	104
Phoenix	Bec Woods	105
The Most Beautiful Smile	Marilyn Pemberton	106
No Laughing Matter	Bec Woods	107
The Big Guns	Margaret Mather	111
For Rory with love	Jackie Skipp	118
Just Bricks and Mortar	Ann Evans	119
Ribbons	Marilyn Pemberton	128
The Rose Vase	Ann Evans	129
The Lake	Marilyn Pemberton	134
Lover's Lake	Mary Ogilvie	135
Crackpot	Bec Woods	136
One Summer's Evening	Marilyn Pemberton	138
Plenty of Fish	Maxine Burns	139
The Door	Catherine Wilson	142
Unlocked	Ella Cook	144
Attack	Ann Evans	146
Family Secrets	Margaret Mather	147
1967: The Summer of Love	Maxine Burns	149
In Deep and Troubled Water	Jackie Skipp	154
Fairy Tales	Margaret Mather	161
Man and Dog V Wind	Marilyn Pemberton	163
Evenings on Abersoch Beach	Catherine Wilson	165
A Siren's Call	Mark Howland	166
A Problem Solved	Catherine Wilson	174
My Favourite Thing	Marilyn Pemberton	177
Every Breath	Maxine Burns	179
Hooked	Bec Woods	182
The King and I	Margaret Mather	184
A Game of Kings	Marilyn Pemberton	189
Stranger in the Park	Ella Cook	195
Meet the Authors	Biographies	204

INTRODUCTION

Welcome to the latest collection of short stories, flash fiction, poetry and articles from the Wordsmiths. We are a group of writers based around Coventry, Nuneaton and surrounding areas who meet regularly for creative writing classes run by myself – Ann Evans, a writer of some 30 years and author of over 32 books and many articles.

The Wordsmiths are a delightfully mixed group of published and unpublished writers – who all share a passion for writing. This shows in the wide variety of styles and themes in our collection. We hope there will be some that you will love.

Often in classes, I'll set the students writing exercises which result in some surprising pieces of work. Some of these are included in this anthology, along with a brief explanation of what the class exercise entailed.

Some pieces are quite sinister and may send a shiver down your spine, some may bring a tear to your eye, while others are sure to bring a smile to your face.

So, grab a coffee or tea and maybe a slice of cake, sit back, relax and enjoy some unique stories, flash fiction and poetry from our little gang of enthusiastic writers.

Ann Evans

THE SHADOW

By Marilyn Pemberton

The theme for this story by Marilyn was 'Shadows'.

She was late. She'd never get home by 10 o'clock and she knew her father would carry out his threat to ground her for a month if she was so much as a minute past the deadline. She walked as fast as her high heels would allow – to run would be folly.

She knew this part of town well and at first, she rushed past the entrance, for the alley had been out of bounds for as long as she remembered. "Don't ever, ever, go down there, do you understand Sarah? It's not safe. Promise me you'll never, ever go down there." And she had kept her promise to her mother up until now, but she realised that it was a short-cut that would mean she could get home on time.

She didn't waste any more time prevaricating and her heels clattered on the cobble stones as she hurried down the alley. A neon light about half-way down suddenly sprang to life and she could see inside what seemed to be antique shops, whose ugly, dusty artefacts were just placed higgledy-piggledy in the bow windows. As she neared the flickering neon light her 'phone buzzed. Never one to leave a text unanswered she stopped, quickly read the message from her best friend and sent a reply: *on way hm, call later.*

As her fingers flew over the keys, she saw something move on the floor by her feet. She hated rats so stepped back and was bemused when she saw that the movement was caused by a shadow, seemingly detaching itself from her and walking slowly away. She spun round to see who else was behind her, but there was no-one there. Her shadow had been with her every day of her 16 years and she knew it was hers, but how could it be? Her puzzlement grew as the shadow threw the shadow-phone to the floor and put its shadow-hands to its shadow-throat.

Sarah's puzzlement turned to terror as she suddenly felt a band around her neck. She dropped the 'phone and clawed at her throat but felt nothing there, just a pressure that squeezed and squeezed, preventing her drawing breath. Her lungs burned for want of air and she fell to her knees, as did her shadow, its hands still grasping its neck.

In just a few minutes, Sarah's lifeless body slumped to the ground, as did her shadow.

The neon light gave one final sputter then went out. Sarah's shadow, now undetectable in the dark of the unlit alley, slithered away over the ancient cobbles.

SHADOWS

By Mark Howland

Another 'Shadow' themed piece of work, in a dialogue only structure.

SHOP OWNER: Welcome to 'Shadow lands', how may I help you, Sir?

CUSTOMER: I would like to return my shadow.

SO: I see, and may I enquire as to the problem?

C: My shadow casts no shadow, I believe it to be shy.

SO: Well, Sir, it's what they do, wouldn't be much of a shadow if it cavorted out in the open now would it, shadows are sly by their very natures.

C: I didn't say sly, I said shy.

SO: Oh, I see. Maybe it's just a performance issue, why not give it a little while longer to settle in, and if it still fails to make an appearance, we will happily offer a replacement or a full refund, no quibbles, whichever you choose.

C: I'm afraid that simply will not do. I have an important conference to attend in three days, and I am the shadow speaker. It is imperative that my shadow is seen.

SO: Can't you just, dim the lighting? Or perhaps linger in the shadows that do work?

C: Out of the question! I am a vampire hunter by trade, a person that casts no shadow is one of the distinguishing characteristics of a vampire. I wouldn't be much of a vampire hunter if I didn't cast a shadow, now would I?

SO: Hmmmm, I see your point. Well, if you pop upon this pedestal, my unworthy assistant will remove the faulty one while you peruse our catalogue for a replacement.

C: What do you mean catalogue?

SO: If you will excuse me for just a moment, Sir. Snipe! Come here, come here and stop flinching, you wretch of a man! Did you sell this customer his faulty shadow?

SNIPE: Yes, my beloved keeper of shades.

SO: Stop grovelling at once! Did you not provide him with the catalogue, and the full service we are proud to provide?

SNIPE: I didn't, spare me please 'o' gracious one.

SO: And why not? You defiler of decency.

SNIPE: Because I was wearing a shadow of doubt on that particular day.

SO: Snipe, go and fetch us a pot of tea, and don't forget to boil your head too, preferably in a separate pan!

SNIPE: Thirty seconds, my divine merchant of shadiness?

SO: Sixty. Now, where was I? Yes, the catalogue! If I may take your measurements, please, Sir.

C: Look, will this take long, I have an appointment this evening I cannot afford to miss. Is there not a 'one size fits all' or something?

SO: We cannot afford to rush this I'm afraid. I once had a gentleman like you, looking for a new shadow. Most impatient he was; his shadow had got lost in a crowd, presumably ended up as a coffee shop lamp shade. Anyway, I had sewn on a medium size, but he had unusually small feet. He was jubilant for a short while, as his shadow gave him extra inches added to his shoes. Shortly after, while hunting in the Congo, he misjudged stepping over a sleeping lion. Ironically, all that was left uneaten were his tiny loafers.

C: This is absurd, I have heard quite enough of this nonsense, besides, the writer has now exceeded five hundred words. Good day, Sir!

SO: Oh well, I guess it's just me, and my shadows.

SNIPE: And Snipe, Sir!

SO: And Snipe...

SHADOW

By Mary Ogilvie

Some thoughtful pieces of writing from Mary

She knew it was there, always behind her. Like a guardian angel following her about. She could not lose it. It would not go, or move without her, leaving her to be alone.
It had started at birth and grown with her. Forever lurking, but never imposing or intruding in her life.
She took it for granted, never questioning or acknowledging its presence. Its silence never gave her cause to complain.
Her shadow and her were one together, but should she give it another name?

PASSION

Slowly, silently, He makes his way ahead. Surrounded by followers and an angry mob baying for His blood. But He remains steadfast, accepting their ignorance. And the cross which He carries becomes a symbol of His love, and the sacrifice He made for others.

SMILE

A smile can cover a multitude of sins.
A smile can brighten, enlighten any day.

THE KNOCK

By Ann Evans

'Shadows' inspired this story too.

I'm expecting a knock on the door any day now. I know it's coming. I can feel it – sense it. It's bound to happen now that I ain't on the move anymore. The shadows of my past are catching up on me. Dark shadows in some cases.

It weren't easy, growing up in the East End in the fifties. Teddy boys they called us. I had thick black hair then, combed into a quiff and slicked down with Brylcreem; and crepe-soled shoes and drainpipe trousers. But it was the fights I remember most. It was all flick knives in those days. Flick knives and gangs. You had to be tough, you'd got no chance if you didn't show them who was boss.

Now don't get me wrong, I ain't never killed no-one. I don't think so anyway. But quite a few would like to get their hands on me. Plenty of the thugs I've encountered swore to get me, make me pay. So, I kept on the move.

Until now, that is. They put me in this old folks' home. It's nice. Trouble is, its permanent. My name's logged into them bloody computers now. Name, date of birth, place you were born. All there for anyone to see – and come and get me.

It's gonna happen. Them shadows are getting closer every day. I'd always been able to keep one step ahead. Even the coppers couldn't catch me. They've got a list as long as my arm, they have, of stuff I've done. The last misdemeanour was not turning up in court to account for all my other misdemeanours.

I thought they'd track my down in no time. I guess I was better at ducking and diving than I thought 'cos they never came knocking at my door – not any of my doors. I kept on the move. Stay in a town just long enough to have a bit of fun. Upset a few people – I didn't mean to. It was just my way I suppose. When things started to get a bit edgy, I'd head off to pastures new. So, the coppers never caught up with me.

Got no place to run to now though. I don't really want to go to prison, not now, not at my age. I know I ain't been no saint – far from it. But like I said, I ain't never killed no one, and I ain't one of them perverts neither, fiddling with little kiddies. I never did any of that. Turns my stomach that does. Nah, it's always been the ladies for me.

One special lady. Don't know if she's still alive. I like to think she is. Alicia! That was her name. I was twenty-two, she was twenty, and I loved her with all of my heart, adored her, worshiped the ground she walked on. And she felt the same. Only when you're that young you're a bit vulnerable to the charms of other ladies. And one night I did the dirty on her, I'm ashamed to say. I messed about with another young lady, and low and behold that other young lady, Maureen, ended up, up the duff.

I didn't get on my bike quick enough that time. I hung around trying to get Alicia to forgive me. She cried a lot. I'd broken her heart, smashed it into smithereens. She didn't forgive me. She said I ought to do the right thing and marry Maureen, make an honest woman out of her. Take care of the baby.

So, I did that, married Maureen, brought our son up 'till he was three-and-a-half, and I loved him. Really loved that little chap. But Maureen was hell. I'd have murdered her if I'd stayed. She drove me nuts. But I never lifted a finger against her, never. But I had to go before I did. It broke my heart leaving our little boy. We'd named him Charlie.

Sometimes I dream about that knock on the door. That the shadow behind the glass panel would be him, Charlie. That he'd tracked me down 'cos he loved and missed me. Ha! If he did track me down, it would probably be to punch me on the nose for deserting him and his mum. I'd take it though, take anything to see him again.

It wouldn't surprise me if it was Maureen who comes looking, if she's still around. Or the CSA wanting years of alimony. But I dream that it's Alicia's pretty knuckles that will knock on my door one day. If she did, if she'd finally forgiven me, if she still loved me like I still love her, maybe she'd track me down. Trace me on the internet like you can do these days.

Listen to me, wallowing in the past, feeling sorry for myself. My life is of my own making. Whatever shadows come creeping up on me, they're shadows I've created for myself. And I shouldn't moan. Still got my health, still got my good looks – well, a bit craggy these days, but I'm not in bad shape for my age. Still got a lot of my hair too. I don't use that Brylcreem though. Bet they don't even make it these days.

Someone's knocking at my door.

Am I imagining it? All this reminiscing. Talking to myself? Nope, there it goes again. "Okay, I'm coming."

There's a shadow behind the glass panel, and my heart's pounding inside my chest. I could ignore the knock. Tell them to clear off. But my feet seem to have a will of their own. And I stand there at the door, looking at the shadow, afraid suddenly, relieved suddenly, hopeful suddenly...

I open the door.

"Morning, sweetie. Are you coming down to the lounge today? We've got something special to show you."

It's Daphne, one of the carers here at the home. Nice woman, so I smile and follow her down the corridor into the communal lounge. As I follow her, listening to her chatting, I block out my feelings – the fear, the relief, the hope. Block them out like I've always done.

"There!" Daphne says, sitting me down in front of one of them computer things, and grinning. "We have three new computers. We're going to bring you old sweeties into the 21st century!"

Two other residents are sat alongside of me, we're all looking at these screens like they're going to bite us.

"What do we want with these bloomin' things for?" I ask, folding my arms.

Daphne's still smiling her big white smile. "I'm going to introduce you to the internet. Show you how to look and research. See countries you've never been to. Look back at history, learn, visit your past. Trace your ancestors, trace your long, lost friends."

My ears have pricked up. "Trace long lost friends?"

"Sure, all you need it their name, date of birth, place they were born."

I can feel something stirring inside of me. A sort of excitement. I wonder if Alicia is still alive. I wonder if she married, had children. I wonder if she's forgiven me. And I wonder about my son, Charlie. What's he done with his life? Where is he? Where's Alicia?

I take a deep breath, and putting my fingers on the keyboard, I look up at Daphne and say, "So what do I do first?"

MY TIME

By Margaret Mather

A sad story inspired by 'Shadows' from Margaret

"Show yourself, let me see your face," I cry, desperately peering into the mist, swirling and dancing before my eyes. Playing hide-and-seek with my mind, it races towards hidden corners and sits there, waiting to be found.

Grey, shadowy figures fill the room, talking amongst themselves in hushed voices. I wish I could understand them. Do they talk about me? Oblivious to my calls for help, they continue to whisper, and I realise I cannot be heard. Salt-laden tears sting, as they splash unhindered onto my dry, cracked lips. I'm not afraid. The silhouette holding my hand comforts me, although I sense its grief.

Trying to lift my head is an effort, I fail and a sigh escapes from my parched mouth. Conversation abruptly stops. Gentle fingers take my pulse. I am not yet dead.

The image holding my hand fades as an impenetrable fog descends upon my mind. Lurking in all parts of my brain, it bides its time. I long to know who, or what, hides there. Maybe I should be scared but it doesn't feel menacing, just- edgy. I don't want to prod its depths, I'm not ready. Dragging my jumbled thoughts away, I gaze at the soft, silver aura, surrounding my hospital bed and it calms me.

For a moment, the mist rises, and the room becomes crystal clear.

Cradling our new-born son in his arms, my husband lifts anguished eyes to my face. I yearn to ease his heartache but know it's impossible. Gently, he places our son on the bed beside me.

Crescent shaped eyebrows, frame inquisitive blue eyes, on a pink flawless face. Dark, silky hair covers a perfectly formed head. Strong arms and legs wriggle impatiently. He is beautiful. I long to touch him, feel his warmth on my breast but the effort is too great.

Without warning, five small fingers, wrap tightly around my outstretched thumb. My heart crumples with love. This singular show of tenderness justifies my decision to stop all treatment.

But now it's too late. Disease has taken my body and is about to devour my mind.

All I have is this moment, with my son.

Bit by bit, my husband and son recedes and all I can see are haphazard shapes. Drab, dismal shapes. "Come back," I scream unnoticed. "Please, come back."

Darkness descends again and lies inside my head like a blackout blind. Frantically, I search for any sign of light and about to give up, notice a small glimmer. Slowly at first, it trickles in, then gathering pace, flows like molten gold and floods my mind with radiance.

In the distance, I see an army of trumpet-like flowers on slender green stems, their petals the colour of sugared almonds. Moving closer, a burst of sweet-smelling perfume, blasts my senses and I know she's come for me.

Edging forward, I recognise the kindly face of my beloved grandmother. Eyes shining with love, arms outstretched in welcome.

Smiling, she beckons, and I am happy to follow, pain free at last.

ERASING HISTORY

By Catherine Wilson

This article by Catherine reminds us to look very carefully at photographs

Open that box of old black and white photographs and look at them carefully. What do you see in that crumpled pile? In my pile I see history.

I sort and scan them, as everyone does, and blow them up on my screen, looking at the backgrounds, the places these pictures were taken, many places which have long gone. That's history.

I look at my old photographs, and those taken by my family and others before me—faded, cracked and folded where they have been lying neglected in drawers and boxes over the years as photography developed, and we and our cameras became more sophisticated.

I found a packet of 1920s photos taken at a christening where the light had got into the camera and burnt out Uncle Bert's face on every picture, and Aunties dress was a blob of white fluff, but the backgrounds were clear. No-one threw them away. In those days, photography was magic, every photo precious.

Early 20th Century – the era when anyone could buy and use a camera, was one of the greatest phenomena of our time. I was looking at some 2 ¼" square photos taken on a 1960's Cornish camping holiday. In the background was a potato peeler which we took with us – a heavy clonking contraption, with a handle on the top; plus our newest claim to camping sophistication – a stove with not one, but two burners, (in spite of the fact that we had no proper fitted groundsheet in the tent—that came later,) These were memories I had quite forgotten until I saw them again in these old pictures

Seeing these backgrounds in the photos evokes memories for me and my family. Being children then, they have different memories to mine. I had also forgotten until reminded by them that the peeler gave up the ghost at John O' Groats a couple of years later. We often wondered what the farmer thought it was, when he saw it sitting on a cowshed wall after we'd left.

Children playing in the garden, we all have those pictures. But "hey," I say, "I'd forgotten about that old pedal car in the background at the old house. I wonder what happened to it. And weren't babies' prams big in those days.

And those awful orange faces in hand coloured wedding photos. One of my favourites was a black and white wedding photo I bought from a car boot sale. It was taken in a backyard. Classic pose, Matriarch grimly sitting on a dining chair at the front and Patriarch standing tightly buttoned into his stiff best suit at her side, the rest of the family arranged formally around them. But what a background.

An old bike leans up against what looks like a privy door, and hanging on the wall, almost touching one of the bridesmaid's shoulders, is a large tin bath. Now whilst I'm not advocating that we should all dash out and buy a tin bath as an essential background prop for our wedding photographs, my point is that far too much cloning goes on now in photographs – often because we can!

We must value this type of social history, much of which is only contained in the normal family snapshot. History which we are in danger of erasing in our effort to create the 'perfect' picture, which often is quite sterile.

So, be careful when you erase unwanted detail. You may be erasing history.

A POETIC EXCUSE

By Bec Woods

If students didn't do their homework, they had to bring a written excuse.

Another week, another letter,
will the situation ever get better?

Will Bec achieve a consistent flow?
Will her writing pipeline ever grow?

Can she find her creative spark?
Or be forever in the dark?

Oh, the drama of long-lost prose,
or dead-beat poems that comatose

Where's the seven-year-old aspiring writer?
What was said that happened to fright her?

Did writer's block stem her thoughts?
The lack of ideas make her fraught?

Or was it laziness, mental inertia,
a lack of discipline that finally caught her?

Perhaps she's trying just too hard,
to achieve perfection, like the Bard.

Whatever caused the creative stun,
Remember Bec writing's supposed to be fun.

ALPHABET OF QUOTATIONS

By Mary Ogilvie

A class exercise the aim was to come up with a memorable quotation. Mary came up with a whole alphabet of them.

A: Always look on the bright side of life
B: Begin at the beginning
C: Capture the moment
D: Do unto other as you would like to be done by
E: Every cloud has a silver lining
F: Figment of the imagination
G: Go where no man has gone before
H: Honesty is the best policy
I: Ignorance is bliss
J: Justice will prevail
K: Knowledge is a great thing
L: Laugh and the world laughs with you
M: Mind over matter
N: Never judge a book by its cover
O: Onwards and upwards
P: Power to the people
Q: Quick as lightning
R: Reach for the stars
S: Sweet dreams
T: Till we meet again
U: You never know until you try
V: Veni, Vidi, Vici (I Came, I Saw, I Conquered)
W: What a day for a daydream
X: X and a hug
Y: You only live once?
Z: Zero

ALPHABETTI

By Maxine Burns

Maxine has written an Acrostic poem using the alphabet.

A village not far from town,
broad river cutting the woods in half.
Calendula and daisies vie for attention,
dying, to be replaced by summer's bounty.
Each wild garlic leaf blowing gently,
frogs grown from spawn
gamble and fly through the mist.
Home is just down this path,
in a copse flooded with dappled light.
Jacket hanging behind the door,
keys ready in my hand and
loneliness bleeds from my soul as
memories revive in my mind.
Never forget who I am
or to what I aspire.
Please don't deny my caress,
quietly lie in my arms and
revive the love we once had.
Sit with me, share a bottle of wine even though
time is written on my face.
Useless to pretend, carry on.
Victory no more, only the grave awaits.
Wanton, this waste of our love,
xcellent though it once was.
You could you not wait for me? So
zealous in your hideous escape.

AN ALPHABET POEM

By Marilyn Pemberton

Letters of the alphabet creating atmosphere

An autumn
breeze rustles the leaves of the
chestnut tree.
Down fall the nuts onto the warm damp
earth, where they lie nestled in the arms of their
fallen brethren.
Gorse bushes, bedecked in yellow,
hidden
inside domes of brambles, their berries
jettisoned to feed the nibbling beasts.
Knights in armour once roamed these paths, with
lances and
mace, arms against the woodland foe.
Nothing breathes,
other than the trees and the few
pigeons, who sit and coo
quietly in the branches,
roosting in the cooling evening air, waiting for the
sun
to set, safe
under the
verdant canopy.
Waiting in their
Xanadu;
yearning for their lost ones, whose cries can still be heard
in the murmurings of the
zephyr.

WHAT'S IN A NAME?

By Alex Bartlett

Twenty-six letters are all we need.

Alex is in a happy mood.
Bethany is feeling down.
Chris is having a blast.
David doesn't care anymore.
Eric is contemplating his next move.
Fiona is feeling beautiful.
Gemma wants to cut her hair off.
Hanna is enjoying her dinner.
Irene is ready for retirement.
Jane can't wait to start the job.
Katie is as high as a kite.
Lizzy can't sleep.
Monica really needs to sleep.
Noel is running as fast as possible.
Oliver is barely able to get off the couch.
Peter is living the dream.
Quinten is ready for the challenge.
Ruth is playing Kandy Crush.
Steve is troubled.
Tony is ready to jump.
Ulrika is hosting the show
Vanessa is travelling the world.
Wendy is buying her first house.
Xavier is up bright and early.
Yule is ready to rock.
Zander has written this poem.

ARCTIC'S NIGHT

By Mark Howland

Crimson snowflakes tangle and heap within my languid form,
Sorrowful, my continuance sputters beneath a glory glimpse,
I must think of them no more.
Hearing the soft creaker-crack of winters settling bed,
I watch my torpid breath thickly dissolve.
Fathomless reaches press down upon me.
Dare I a final love-look?
Dare I gather once more the faces that fill me?
Without hesitation.
Saline stars suspend mid-slide, my gritting, glitter-mask mirroring above.
Fathomless reaches now pull upon me,
And love smiles back,
Nonplussed, pain moves aside.
Without hesitation, I enter Arctic's night...

A KIND OF MAGIC

"Stories have a unique kind of magic. They will choose a writer to champion them, to carry them ever closer to this world with every pen-stroke, until they are immortalised within the hearts and minds of all who read them."
Mark Howland

BEAUTY SPOT

By Margaret Mather

An exercise in creating characters inspired this piece of writing from Margaret.

Auburn hair with flecks of gold, surround her elfin features. It tumbles untamed onto skeletal shoulders. Each natural curl clearly defined. Morning sun streams through the bedroom window, sprinkling individual strands with copper highlights. Drugs have not dimmed its splendour.

I see pain etched deep into her lined face as she turns to look at me. She tries to smile but the effort is too much. Emerald eyes that once sparkled are now dull and full of anguish. Her translucent skin has erupted in an angry, scarlet rash.

Years ago, she'd had a perfect complexion, rose pink and blemish free, apart from one little mole, sitting high upon her cheek bone. Don't fuss, Robbie, she had said, when I'd begged her to see a doctor.

Now, with her misshapen mouth, she struggles to talk. Cruel consequences of a stroke have robbed my wife of her speech and her dignity. Her body may be twisted and her words indistinguishable, but she is still my beautiful Hanna, my lover, soul mate and friend. She gives meaning to my life and is my reason for living.

Standing by the window, I tell her about the birds in the garden, "The woodpecker's here again. He's making good work of those nuts. They're almost gone, greedy chap."

Birds were her passion and as a gifted artist, she'd study them for hours. Her illness has put paid to that.

Placing both hands on the arms of the chair, she struggles to stand. Rushing to her side, I try to help. Love shines from her soulful eyes. Momentarily they twinkle as she thanks me by pressing on my leg. The effort has been enormous, and she flops down, exhausted.

I offer to apply her favourite make-up, she nods acceptance. Unfastening the scruffy, red velvet cosmetics bag, I feel like an intruder. I've watched her open it for the last fifty years, a gift from me on our first Valentine's Day together.

Unscrewing the lid on her cornflower blue eye shadow feels alien to me. It feels like I'm violating something that is hers and hers alone. She taps my hand and winks her approval. Dabbing it onto her eyelids, I follow up with soft brown mascara on her long, thick eyelashes.

With trembling hands, I try to add her raspberry pink lipstick, but she nudges my fingers away. I didn't think. How could she possibly want to outline her distorted lips? What an idiot. I finish by spraying each wrist with her favourite rose-scented perfume.

Sitting perfectly still, she allows me to brush her glorious hair.

Under normal circumstances, my proud, strong, intelligent wife would fight like a tigress to regain her life. But that little beauty spot, sitting high upon her cheek bone, has other ideas. Sneaking unseen, it's flooded her body with rapidly spreading, cancerous cells.

There's no fight left in her. She has nothing more to give.

Soon, the pills will take her from me.

Holding hands, we sit, and we wait.

MUSIC NEVER FORGETS

By Ella Cook

The class challenge was to write a story using 3 random words: Piano, Beast, Clown.

The piano sat silently in the corner of the room, gathering dust and memories. Every so often someone, usually Alice, would trail a finger along the locked lid, leaving a wistful trail of hope that uncovered the battered wood.

Once upon a time it had been a source of joy and laughter, but now only served to remind everyone of what they had lost. Music was long gone, although some of the residents still rocked and jiggled to songs unheard outside of the confines of their own heads.

It was too disruptive. That was what the doctors, in their wisdom, had claimed – and the key had vanished – along with the hope and joy that it had brought to so many. Some claimed they could remember it being played, of it being covered with tinsel and spouting joyful carols – but their minds were so addled by the beast that held them hostage and devoured their histories, they may well have been remembering a dream or television show. It certainly was more likely than the idea of the dented old piano being used in that place.

Alice sat in the corner, pushed up close to a craft table covered in glue and coloured tissues. Supposedly arts and crafts helped to keep the beast at bay and hold memories intact. But instead of creating memory scrap books that should have reminded her who she was, Alice stared into space, her fingers fluttering across the table.

Norman sat beside her. Ever the clown, he twisted the coloured tissues in an approximation of flowers, and dotted them in Alice's hair, laughing to himself as he tucked them into her platinum curls. Alice paid no heed, her fingers still dancing and tapping out rhythms through the crafting flotsam.

Then finally, one day, a miracle happened. As was typical in this place it was proceeded by sadness. Another resident making their final trip, never to return. But as the family had cleared away the final sad reminders of a life forgotten – it was found. A tiny, uninspiring brass key that, with a bit of wriggling and Ponds cold cream as lubrication – finally released the music again.

Alice's fingers had shaken as she'd wandered aimlessly towards the rows of black and white keys, and slowly stroked one or two. After a moment of hesitation in which her addled mind fought to recover some secret, she smiled to herself and pulled up a chair.

Within moments, Norman's tissue flowers cascaded around her as muscles took over and provided the memories her mind had forgotten, and music and sunlight filled the air.

MAM

By Maxine Burns

The class exercise was to make a story from these 3 random words: Tankard, Best Friend, Taught.

The tankard had been on the sideboard for as long as I could remember. Right at the back, behind the letter rack that Mam kept all her bills in. It was so familiar that I'd never really thought about it, certainly never held it in my hands. I do know that there was always some money in it. 'Just in case,' Mam use to say as she dropped a few pennies in it. Then we'd laugh, although to be honest, I wasn't sure why.

It was a silver colour, and as the years passed it had blackened in places. It was just there, you know. Like the house itself, like the greasy old cooker which stood in the tiny cold kitchen, like Mam herself.

I've always considered Mam my best friend. Odd you'd say, for a man to have his mam as his best friend. Sad, you'd say. Your mam is your best buddy! What about school, what about your job? Who do you go out for a drink with? Truth is, the boys at school didn't like me. Bullied they'd call it today. Character building, they called it then. Our teacher would say, 'Stand up to them, be a man.'

I've always worked alone. I like it that way. Tending the garden up at the big house. Caring for the plants, pruning, weeding, and mowing the lawn. Watering the tender young lettuces.

Mam sorted those boys at school for me. You should have heard her. And she got me the job I love so much. She does everything for me. Buys my clothes, cooks my meals and much more. Like I said, Mams my best friend.

Mam taught me everything. How to eat, how to walk. Where to shit. When not to shit. Now, I've absolutely no idea what to do. If I've been in the kitchen once, I've been a dozen times. The food is there, potatoes, cabbage, small single portions of ready meals in the freezer. I could even prepare it. All should be good.

But I can't figure the cooker out. The gas won't light. I can hear it hissing out of the little round holes but when I light the match it goes out. I've eaten the cabbage and all the bread. Everything that you can eat raw is gone.

I've asked Mam what I should do at least a dozen times. She's in bed. I've shaken her but she won't wake up and she's very cold and she needs a bath. Mam didn't like the neighbours, and as I've said, I've got no friends. I really don't know what to do.

Mam, wake up.

DAD

By Maxine Burns

A follow-on story from Maxine. The 3 random words this time being: Snake, Candlewax, Paragon.

My sister was always interested in snakes. An unhealthy interest, I thought. Dad thought it was great. 'Shows an inquiring mind,' he said. Me and Mum thought it was just creepy. He even let her have one, then another. Before we knew it there were vivariums all over the place. Libby and Dad would swan off to somewhere in Europe, then come back with one or two new ones every time. 'Great bond we have, me and Libby,' he'd say.

It wouldn't have been quite so bad, but a number of them were poisonous, deadly in fact and Mum and I had to feed them whilst they were away. There was a special fridge (thank God,) that the food was stored in. Dead mice and rats, Ugh! Mum had put her foot down about keeping live ones in cages, breeding them for food. (Thank God.)

One night there had been a power cut, so we had to feed them by candlelight. Mum put on the thick rubber gloves and held the snake hook threateningly as she opened each glass box and dropped a stiff, cold body inside. I felt sick as the snakes lunged towards them so concentrated on the candlewax as it dripped gloopily down the candlesticks.

Libby and Dad returned late that night. Libby was buzzing, there was no new snake, (thank god,) as she had met some bloke on the train. They'd spent all day together (and probably the night, knowing Libby,) although she didn't say. Dad was fuming, he had a right face on him.

Mum opened a bottle of wine to go with supper and we all sat round the kitchen table to hear all about it. As soon as dad had finished, he took his glass to the sitting room and put the football on so loud that mum had to get up to close the door. Libby couldn't stop talking about this paragon, Piers, (Piers?) He was tall, he was blonde, he was gorgeous and apparently was going to put a ring on it, she said, waggling the third finger of her left hand.

I rolled my eyes at Mum and went to join Dad, but he was glued to the TV and I couldn't get a word out of him, so I went to bed with a book.

I was up early the next morning and went downstairs to make a cup of tea. Libby was already up. I could hear her talking softly to her snakes. I peeked around the door and asked if she wanted a drink. I could see she had been crying. "What's up?" I asked, walking to her albeit gingerly as she was transferring a snake, (the mamba?) to a cage so that she could clean its home.

"'It's dad," she said. He'd refused to allow Piers (Piers!) to come for a visit the next weekend. "He doesn't like him," Libby wailed.

She was in a right old state, not fit to be handling lethal snakes, so I sat her down and we talked as I cleaned the vivarium, wrinkling my nose at the disgusting mess on the bottom.

"So why do you think Dad doesn't like, (I paused,) Piers?" And Libby shrugged, she wasn't sure, she said. I dipped the cloth into the water and began to rub at the glass sides. The snake watched me, flicking its tongue. Libby's snakes don't like me (mutual.)

Libby was still crying and even though her eyes were red, and tears were streaming down her face she was still really pretty. "God, Lib," I said, "it can't be that bad, surely, Dad will come around. And you've only known that bloke for a couple of days."

"Dad will never let me go," she said.

I looked at her. "What do you mean?"

She looked at me. "Don't pretend you don't know," she said in a really cold voice. Not like Libby at all.

The vivarium was clean, sparkling in fact. I took the snake hook off the wall and pulled on the protective gloves.

She stood. "I'll do it."

I ignored her, opened the cage and took out the snake, holding it firmly at the neck. I turned to face Libby who was standing quite close. The snake flicked its tongue, furiously. Libby looked at it, almost mesmerized. I dipped it a little closer. She looked at me and smiled.

I stepped back and returned the snake to its home. Maybe tomorrow, I thought.

PANCHO

By Catherine Wilson

A family pet inspired this poem from Catherine

There once was a cat named Pancho who came in from the rain,
One night it was, she looked around and made it her domain.
For twenty years she ruled the roost, including thirteen rabbits.
This gorgeous, dainty, tortoise shell, had hidden nasty habits.
A thief she was, so devious, all food they had to hide,
Undaunted, she chose a neighbour's house and sneaked herself inside.
A pack of ham she gobbled up, and custards on a plate.
Suddenly she heard a noise, it was the garden gate.

Silently she came back home and lay down on her mat.
Neighbour scratched her head surprised but didn't blame the cat.
Until the day when she was spied and chased out of the door
A pound of sausage trailing and dropped down on my floor.
Neighbour was not happy, an understatement that.
He swore that if it came again he'd shoot the blasted cat.
Peace reigned awhile till Pancho had three kittens in their shed
And some months later had four more, upon same neighbour's bed.

We then moved house and things were fine, for a while at least.
She ate the neighbour's guinea pigs, a gory royal feast.
On moving day the hiding cat got stuck inside a drain.
The firemen tried to tempt her out, but it was all in vain.
Slabs were lifted, garden trashed but she went further in.
We stopped for tea; on coming back, she sat there on the bin.
Nineteen years in cat years, one thirty-three in ours
Pancho our little character, sleeps safe beneath the flowers.

THE BLUE BENCH

By Margaret Mather

A photo of a park bench inspired Margaret to write this short story.

The ground was crisp underfoot as Annie and her husband Michael started their walk. Tree branches dripping with icicles bowed under the weight of an unexpected hoar frost and surrounding fields shimmered in the winter sun.

Annie loved the peace and quiet of this magical winter wonderland and was soon striding out. Michael, with his head bent, collar turned up against the cold and hands shoved deep into his pockets, trailed behind.

"Come on slow coach, the faster you walk the warmer you'll feel." Annie shouted as she disappeared around a bend in the path.

She worried about her husband. He'd changed, become a grumpy old man overnight. They used to laugh at the silliest things, sharing a similar sense of humour.

She remembered how Michael had looked forward to giving up work for good. He'd ticked the days off on a calendar, well in advance of the due date. He'd tease workmates with tales of lying in bed all day while they toiled from dawn to dusk.

The first three months weren't too bad. Michael spent most of his time in the garden. He painted the summer house, the shed, the decking and anything else that needed it.

Running out of things to refurbish, Michael immersed himself in crazy paving. Thankfully the weather changed, and the paving stopped.

Turning his attention to birds of the feathered variety, he bought feeders in all shapes and sizes and sat in the summerhouse, for hours on end, photographing them.

She'd been pleased that he'd managed to keep himself occupied but as soon as winter surfaced, she'd noticed a difference in him. He never smiled or cracked a joke. All he had wanted to do was sit and stare at the television. She was tired of his ill-tempered remarks.

Today she hoped would be different. A brisk walk in open countryside ending at the pub by the river would do them both the world of good. She stopped and waited for him to catch up.

"What's that up there on the hill?" Annie asked pointing to a structure in the distance.

"How would I know? It's been ages since we walked this route. It looks like some sort of shrub to me," he replied scuffing his boots on the path and blowing into his hands in a vain attempt to keep them warm.

"I'm freezing, can we go home now?"

Annie ignored his pleas. "Why don't we investigate, it'll only take ten minutes. You can borrow my gloves if you're that cold."

She took her pink woollen mitts of and offered them to her husband. He waved her hand away. There was a time he would have laughed and accepted her offer graciously.

The crunching of their feet on the frosted trail was the only sound they shared. Slightly out of breath but much warmer, they reached the brow of the hill. To Annie's delight, a bench made from wrought iron and painted cornflower blue, sat by the side of the path. Two dolphins, riding the waves, were carved on the back. The position of the seat overlooked the river, beyond lay silver coloured patchwork fields, stretching for miles. It felt serene and

Annie sat down to rest, wondering who the seat was 'in memory' of.

On the grass by the side of the bench, lay a faded flower wreath, made up from letters that spelled: MUM. A glass vase standing nearby held a single red rose. It was a wistful moment as Annie contemplated who this poor woman had been.

"Can we go now?" Michael asked. "I think it's going to snow, look at the sky."

Annie looked up at the clear blue sky and wondered where Michael had picked up his weather forecasting skills.

"It doesn't look like snow to me. Have a look in that pot and see if there's any information on this lady," Annie said, pointing to a brown plastic plant pot, lying wedged underneath the bench.

"Bit nosey if you ask me," Michael said stooping to retrieve the pot.

"I'm curious. I'd like to know the name of the woman who shared my enjoyment of this special view."

Peering into the pot Michael found a piece of laminated paper. Lifting it out and holding it up to the light he said, "Her name was Sally Missel."

"Sally Missel," Annie repeated. "'Well, that's an unusual name if ever there was one."

"See for yourself," he said, thrusting the piece of paper at Annie.

Taking her glasses out of her pocket, she put them on. The winter sun was in her eyes and she turned her head away in search of shade. Annie read and re-read the note. Her hands trembled. She was unable to look at Michael, scared she'd lose control. Her shoulders heaved and slowly, a gurgling noise escaped from her clenched mouth.

"What's the matter, Annie? Did you know her? Please, don't upset yourself." his face was full of concern.

"I'm not crying, Michael, I'm laughing. You really do need to wear your glasses."

"I don't know what you mean, I can read perfectly well thank you."

"Can you now? All I can read on the note is: To a dear friend – sadly missed."

Annie watched as her husband's face first registered bewilderment, then as realisation dawned, it took on the transformation she'd been longing for. His eyes lit up and a roar of laughter burst from his mouth. The more he laughed the more she did, they couldn't stop.

Once they'd regained their composure, Annie jumped up and shouted, "Race you to the pub."

"Okay, you're on, but only if we share the mitts," he replied, putting his arms around her and kissing her cold cheek.

COMRADES

by Jackie Skipp

A photograph of World War I soldiers in battle trenches inspired this poem.

They were comrades in the beginning, when the Army was a choice.
They were comrades during the halcyon days, when wars were historical events.
They were comrades in training.
They were comrades at play.
They were comrades when war broke out, and the world was afraid.
They were comrades who bade sweethearts and mothers farewell.
They were comrades on the train.
They were comrades on the ship.
They were comrades who dug trenches.
They were comrades who tasted soil and blood and sweat.
They were comrades who buried other comrades.
They were comrades in death.

THIS WAS GOING TO HURT

By Alex Bartlett

This flash fiction story by Alex was prompted by the 3 random words: Happy, Glared, Blanket.

This was going to hurt.

Alistair wasn't sure he wanted to open his eyes yet. His head was pounding, and he felt dehydrated. The alcohol still burned the back of his throat.

With a deep breath, he opened his eyes and saw the light streaming through the half-opened curtains. He winced as the pain in his head shot up dramatically.

He forced his eyes to stay open and lifted the blanket off himself. His head was still spinning.

"How much did I drink last night?" he wondered, looking round the room, seeing clothes and bottles scattered around.

A flashback came into his head from last night: him with bottle of JD in one hand and his friends egging him on to finish it after having had most of it already.

He cursed himself for being so easily led.

He got up and glared at his reflection in the mirror, his hair all over the place and eyes all puffy. He had to stop this and get his life back on track. He knew drinking like this wouldn't make him happy or improve his life.

He'd said this before, and nothing had happened, but this time, it felt different. This time, he was really going to knock the alcohol on the head.

Well, until next weekend at least.

LIVE – HERE!

By Robert Tysall

The 3 random word exercise prompted this piece of flash fiction from Rob. The words being: Live, Late, Church.

'Live!' the poster said. 'Here!' the poster said.

Steve was pleased because this was the band's first gig and it was great to see their name up in lights. He knew he'd picked a brilliant name for the band, calling it: 'Here!'

So many times, he'd seen venues advertising 'Live Here!' and knew it was cheeky but felt people would appreciate the humour. Somewhat similar to: 'Free Beer here!' the band being called 'Free Beer'.

Tonight, would be their first appearance live and he felt confident all was going to flow well. He just hoped the drummer would behave himself.

As the time grew near to go on stage, all the band members had spent time in the changing room, warming up and generally annoying each other. The singer, Tommy, had been doing his usual yodelling – up and down, up and down. The bass player had been sitting there slapping his bass strings to warm his hands up. They keyboard player had been warming up with his namesake, *Jack Daniels.* The drummer, 'Sticks', always warmed up on his rubber pads. And as for himself, sitting and going up and down the guitar frets arpeggio-ing, hammering and generally building up his speed for the event, and making sure they would be ready and dressed for the start of the gig.

Never, ever late on stage.

The concert was a complete success. Everybody had played their part. The audience had seen the funny side of the band and loved their attitude on stage. Steve was now confident he could work this band. And it could only get better and better.

Soon after he'd got off stage he'd been approached by a local agent, eager to book the band. He was glad the boys had agreed to play a mixture of classic, well known songs and also songs they had penned themselves.

It was like a dream coming true, a far cry from those early days playing acoustic guitar with his church choir. Now the future lay firmly in their own hands.

THE PIANO

By Marilyn Pemberton

Three random words inspired this from Marilyn. The words being: Piano, Beast, Clown.

The piano was the first thing to go, it being, so my father said, a luxury we could now ill afford. I was playing Bach when the men came, their grubby overalls taut over their beer-rounded bellies. Their hob-nailed boots clattered on the uncarpeted floorboards and their red calloused hands took hold of her and lifted her as if she was made of paper, even as I continued to play. My father pulled me away and I watched through tears as she was man-handled through the doorway and I cried out loud as she was banged against the walls and into the van.

My fingers, with no notes to play, drummed against my thighs. My father was still holding my arm tightly, as if he thought I would run after her. "Well, that's that. I'm sorry, love, but, well, you know it had to be done."

I suddenly saw him for what he was; a weak man and a failure. I pulled away from him and beat my fist on his thin chest. "I hate you! You're a beast! How am I going to live without her? She was everything to me, you know that!"

He pulled me to him and hugged me tight. "I know, I know. I'm so sorry. I'll get her back when I get a job, I promise. It won't be long."

It was, though. More and more furniture disappeared over the next few weeks and eventually we ended up sitting on the floor, huddled together for warmth.

I saw her once in a second-hand music shop. She was dusty and there were scratches along her side, but it was definitely her. I went in, opened the lid and played a scale. She was tuneless and it made me feel sick with grief and longing. There was a clown plonked on top of her, his grinning face mocking me as his head nodded up and down, up and down; his harsh mechanical laugh more musical than my playing.

NIGHT OF HELL

By Alex Bartlett

A class exercise of 3 random words inspired this sinister flash fiction tale from Alex.

Sue stared into the darkness, not believing what she was seeing. A man, bare-chested and covered in ghastly tattoos was standing by a large crypt chanting the same word again and again.

"Rise, rise, rise!"

He had a black staff with a skull on the end and was rhythmically tapping it on the crypt.

Sue and Pete scurried and hid behind the nearest bush, unable to take their eyes off him.

The crypt was starting to shake, eventually crumbling. A horde of skeletons burst out, some with flesh and clothes still dangling from their bodies.

Sue screamed and ran back from where she'd come.

"Sue!" shouted Pete, sprinting after her.

The tattooed man turned and saw his unexpected guests, completely taken by surprise. However, he gained his composure quickly and shouted at his undead army. "Kill them!"

The skeletons needed no second word and charged after the two of them, eating up the ground like a leopard.

They got to Pete first, hacking him down with a few blows. Sue just about heard him shout her name before he died.

Tears streaming down her face, she ran straight into the road, forcing the nearest driver to slam on his brakes.

"Help me!" she cried, throwing open the passenger side door. "Drive!" She jumped into the car and it shot off.

Settling into her seat, she then looked at the driver properly for the first time.

Her blood ran cold and panic stole her voice as she stared at the tattooed hand gripping the steering wheel.

DEAD END

By Marilyn Pemberton

A wrong turn; no-where to turn.
Better to go on.
But the road suddenly peters out.
A dead end.

They espy a cottage, or the remains of one.
Glass panes broken by the stones of countless boys,
A roof more air than slate.
No-one's home now.

They sit on a log, brushing away insects they cannot name,
And eat their shop-bought Panini.
They relish the sun on their faces and the bird song in their ear
And wonder "what if?"

That afternoon a dream is conceived
As is their one and only progeny.
Their underwear is stained with blood
From the berries they crush in their passion.

The child is a toddler before they can move in.
The house is habitable, but only just.
There is still so much to do that the garden remains untouched.
Waiting.

Then in her fifth year, encouraged by tales of Blytonian adventures,

She dons wellingtons and a sou'wester,
Takes an old broom handle in hand
And sets off to right the wrongs of the world.

There's a stone wall as high as the sky and as wide as the eye can see,
Protected by a forest of thorns
That would stop even a love-sick Prince.
A dead end.

But she is fearless; her stocky legs march on,
Led by her determined chin.
She follows a path only she can see
And reaches the other side unscathed.

The wall that is as high as the sky and as wide as the eye can see,
Has a gap,
child sized.
That invites her in.

She claps her hands in sheer delight,
At the glorious floral display.
At the dog roses, clematis and honey-suckle
That have grown unbound since time untold.

There are five trees in a row,
Branches twisted as if in pain.
The trunks are gnarled and grotesque,
Each has a face of its own.

The child calls out to her Mama,
Who arrives, scratched and bloody,
Who wonders who the wall was meant to keep out,

Or perhaps what it was meant to keep in.

The child prances in the sunshine
Enchanted with the laughter only she can hear.
But even though there is not a cloud in the sky
Mama shivers and hears only sighs.

Mama wants the gap filled
But it never gets done, of course.
So, the child spends each day in the garden,
Playing with ghosts.

She stops sometimes and tilts her head,
As if listening to someone speak.
And she smiles and nods
In agreement with the words only she can hear.

One night, Mama finds an empty bed
And a space where slippers should lie
And she is filled with a nameless dread,
She knows not why.

When she squeezes through the gap,
She sees her child standing stock-still.
Torch-light flitting from tree to tree,
As if searching, searching.

mama calls out but it's as if she has made no sound,
For the child seems to be listening to someone else
So intent does she stand, head tilted.
Hearing voices from the dead.

Each tree has a face of its own;
In the torchlight they look almost demonic.

Their open mouths like the entrance to hell
Waiting to draw her angel in.

Mama pulls her child away
From the clutches of the grasping arms
And the silence of the night is shattered by diabolic screams
That only she can hear.

The child ails and worsens day by day
Until she breathes her last.
And like the seed from whence she grew
She is planted in the soil for all eternity.

They visit the garden one last time.
But Mama cannot put a foot inside
And runs away, holding hands to ears
To shut out her daughter's cries.

It is Papa who stands awhile,
Listening to the wind in the trees.
And he counts one, two, three, four, five.
Surely before there were never six?

RAIN OR SHINE

By Robert Tysall

The weather had to be included in this writing exercise, and it inspired this piece of flash fiction from Rob.

I was so happy with the weather today. The roses looked particularly blooming in the garden. The compost was working well.

It's funny but true, especially concerning people in this neighbourhood, or those wanting to buy into it, looking at property was always best done when people could see not only the inside, but the outside of the property too.

And this particular buyer was very keen on number 666 Scythe Road. My house.

I had been working indoors making sure things looked prim and proper when there was a loud knock at the door.

Now I'm a big man, well over 6 feet, but as this man came through the door, he had to bend down to save knocking his head.

"Hello!" I said. "My name's Johnny Walker."

"Good to meet you," he replied. "Thank you for meeting me here at such short notice. My name is Dyer... Dyer Straits."

Rather taken aback by the name, and the appearance of this man – at least 6 foot 7 inches, dressed from head to toe in black, with pale grey skin and bloodshot eyes, I decided to get his viewing over as fast as I could.

After looking over the whole of the property, he was very keen to put forward an offer. This I was happy with. I asked Mr Straits if he would like to sit for a while and I could make him a drink.

He liked straight whisky.

This was definitely one of my favourite choices as well because it hid the taste of certain poisons that you put in it.

As I handed him the drink, I was already plotting out his place in my back garden.

Nobody would be buying my house – not today, not any day. Whether it's sunny or not.

STAR SOURCE

By Alex Bartlett

Alex gives a glimpse into his space story.

The spaceship Star Source was travelling round a remote planet 90 lights years from Earth with its intrepid crew of 40 men, women and robots in the year 2184. Its mission was to locate habitable planets and the Captain, Joseph Harmer, was particularly keen on this one.

It was a beautiful world with a bright, yellow and blue atmosphere; rocky mountains and some water sources. Joseph and his crew had located this planet many years before, but now seeing it with the naked eye, it was even more spectacular than they'd imagined.

This was the day they would step foot on this alien world and see for real if it was a potential human home.

Earth was a dying planet, with pollution making many parts uninhabitable. The 13 billion people on it were starving and living in crowded cities. Humans had to leave Earth before the problem became even worse.

Captain Joseph knew the pressure he and his crew were under for the sake of humanity. He felt sweat trickling down his neck as he got into his space suit.

He was joined by his lieutenant and good friend Kieran Goodman, and one of the ship's robots called G1FT or Gift as people called him. He was humanoid in shape, with grappling claws for arms and wheels for legs.

The three of them walked through the space hatch at the rear of Star Source, a massive, solid door, which closed smoothly behind them. They entered their small pod which would glide them down to the surface.

ABOUT A CAT

By Catherine Wilson

They found you at the bus stop in the bin.
scraggy mog with unmatched staring eyes.
The soaking fur made bones show through your skin.
How could we all resist your plaintive cries.

We brought you home and loved you from that day
A tortoiseshell with absurd velvet ears.
Remember how we taught you how to play
And climb the trees to allay all your fears.

For eighteen years you clung to every heart.
Our feline friend from destination 'bin'
We sorrowed when your time came to depart
And watched as moggy heaven let you in.

Sleep well dear friend beneath your favourite tree.
Leaving holes in our hearts where you should be.

THE HUNT

by Maxine Burns

Creating atmosphere was the inspiration behind Maxine's story.

I look out of the window. It is getting dark. The streetlight is broken; the teenagers who hang about the green have smashed it. I've phoned the council but have had no joy.

My cat sits on the windowsill and looks out into the darkening night with me. She is purring quietly and seems pleased to be on this side of the glass. Like me, she knows it is going to snow and she doesn't like it. She will wait and watch, on the threshold and dab one paw, delicately into the soft white cold, then shocked, she will rush back into the warm and curl up by the fire with a sigh.

I like the snow. It cleans the world. I can look out of the window in the morning, to a picture postcard scene and my heart lifts, as I observe the majestic trees, the hedges and the green, snowy, beautiful, gleaming in winter sunlight.

Through the darkness the cat and I see the first flake. Then another. Her ears and tail twitch with irritation. I sigh with pleasure, pull my chair closer and watch as it falls faster, thicker, till my garden is covered and the path a memory

I hurry into the kitchen to make some cocoa. The cat pads beside me. I put the milk on the stove to heat when it happens. An almighty bang, cracking and the kitchen window dissolves, tinkling onto the stone floor.

The cat screams and bolts. Her paws are bleeding. I am shaking and my breath is caught in my throat. The snowflakes, thicker than ever, gently, softly drift in and settle on the sill. Then I hear the calls. At first, a single voice, quickly joined by others. Soon a dark choir of voices fill the green, chanting, rhythmically. ‘Witch, Witch, kill the Witch. Witch, Witch kill the Witch.’

Goosebumps rise on my arms and cold sweat runs down my back. The cold is pouring in through the shattered glass. The cat, crouched low, limps toward me. I look at her sadly. Soon they will come. I hope they don’t hurt her. ‘Run,’ I say and clap my hands. ‘Run.’ I stamp my foot; she leaps onto the sill and turns to look at me. Are those tears in her eyes?

Then, my lovely girl is gone. Her black body at first stark against the snow, then she melts into the night.

The voices approach. I sit on my chair, with my cocoa, and wait.

THE DUNGEON

by Marilyn Pemberton

The class exercise was to create atmosphere within a dungeon setting.

The early morning sun peeped through the bars in the dungeon window, shining onto Sir Henry's eyes and waking him from his last night's sleep, before his eternal sleep at the hand of the hangman later that day.

He lay on his back on the hard floor; any other position caused his tortured body such excruciating pain. Motes of dust danced in the sunbeam and he imagined himself as one, floating towards his darling Ellen and their child, being there to comfort and protect them, as was his duty and his right.

He heard a terrible thud and knew that the hangman was testing the gallows with a sandbag, making sure that the trapdoor would open to receive his body - but not his spirit. No! Never his spirit! He rolled onto his side and forced himself onto his feet.

He grasped the bars of the window and tried to shout, but his mouth was dry, and he only managed a dry rasp: "Damn you King John, I will see you in Hell!"

TWO OF A KIND

by Mary Ogilvie

The class were tasked to write a Christmas themed story.

"Jess, those boots are way beyond our price range," Megan said as she tried to reason with her daughter over the kitchen table. "And anyway, the heels are far too high for you to wear. You'll fall over and break your neck."

Megan had tried to coax Jess into having a more suitable Christmas present. The 13-year-old's face was red and puffy from crying.

"You just don't want me to have them. It's not fair. Everybody has boots," Jess cried.

"Yes, but do you realise your list is endless?" Megan replied. "And you want tickets for that boy band concert as well."

"So? You've only got me to buy for. Oh! You spoil everything," Jess answered back.

"But that's the point," Megan tried to explain to her daughter, "I don't want to spoil you."

"Fat chance of that," she snapped back at her mother, storming out of the kitchen. She slammed the door shut behind her and stamped her way upstairs.

Megan sat down in the chair and sighed. She hated falling out with her daughter, but her demands were getting ridiculous. Jess was a much-wanted child. She and Ralph had been delighted when she was born. She was the apple of their eye and had never been short of love.

Ralph was a good provider and Jess had never wanted for anything. But now as a 13-year-old teenager with different needs, and expensive tastes, a happy medium was needed.

Megan and Ralph wanted their daughter to

appreciate the value in receiving and not to expect to get everything she wanted just because her friends with more well-off parents did.

It was time to prepare the evening meal. It was Jess's favourite tonight, shepherd's pie. They usually all sat down as a family and enjoyed this time of day together. However, with Jess in such a mood, Megan wondered whether she would be in better spirits by then.

Megan glanced at the kitchen clock. Ralph would be home soon from the allotment. Feeling exhausted from dealing with a teenage daughter, Megan sat down for a well-earned cuppa and a glance at the newspaper. Flicking through the pages, a small advert caught her attention. As she read it with interest it set her thinking about her dilemma with Jess.

"Hi love, look what we've got today."

Looking up she was greeted by Ralph holding a box of newly dug vegetables. She smiled. "You've been busy, love."

"Nice and fresh for our Christmas dinner," said Ralph as he pulled off his mud-covered boots and sat down. "Where's Jess?"

Megan's eyes averted to the ceiling and looking across at Ralph, she gave a pained sigh.

"So, the boots episode didn't go down too well then, I presume," he enquired.

"No," sighed Megan, "Jess doesn't appreciate the value of anything, I wonder does she realise how much we give her, because there seems to be no end to her asking."

Ralph shook his head. "Perhaps we have spoilt her a bit."

Megan nodded, then passed the newspaper she had been reading across to Ralph and pointed at what had caught her attention.

Putting his glasses on, Ralph read in bold black print, the words, 'The Ultimate Christmas Present.'

Looking at Megan, Ralph half smiled, and pausing for thought, tapped his fingers thoughtfully on his chin.

The next day with a list in hand, Megan set about her Christmas shopping. As she paused by the shoe shop window and looked in, there stood the black leather boots that Jess so desperately wanted. Yes, they did look overly stylish for a young girl as well as being overly priced, but Megan decided with a sigh that maybe she would get the boots for Jess, but not everything she wanted.

The smell of mince pies drifted through the house on Christmas Eve. Jess hadn't mentioned the boots again after their argument over them. But now bought they were wrapped up along with the other few presents – plus an extra one that she hadn't asked for.

The lights on the Christmas tree sparkled, and as Megan laid the presents beneath the tree, she held the last of them, a red envelope, close, and hoped with all her heart for the magic of the season to cast its spell.

Next morning the house was a hive of activity as the cooking of Christmas dinner got underway. With relatives arriving to spend the day with them, there was a festive atmosphere of cheer and goodwill.

Everyone complimented Megan on her cooking, and Ralph holding centre stage carving the turkey, looked a treat in his Santa Claus hat. Yuletide carols played in the background and the sound of pulling crackers rang in the air. There was so much family gossip to catch up on during the meal that the day was slipping by quickly.

After they had washed-up after dinner, everyone

began to gather round the tree, and as Megan caught Ralph's eye, they both looked at Jess in anticipation.

There were squeals of delight and laughter as the presents were given out, and one by one opened with curiosity and excitement.

Jess was delighted with her gifts, especially the boots, then looked in eager anticipation at the red envelope addressed to her. She quickly tore the envelope open, but her smile turned to horror as she read its contents.

"Tell me this is a joke," she blurted out in disbelief.

Megan glanced at Ralph as she answered that it was not.

"If you're expecting me to splodge around a smelly donkey sanctuary in these boots, never," wailed Jess.

Megan put her arm around her daughter. "We wanted to give you something special. The latest arrival at the sanctuary isn't mixing with the other donkeys very well, and no one as yet, has adopted her. She could do with a friend, Jess. I'm sure she would appreciate your love and attention which in giving as well as receiving, is what Christmas is all about."

"I don't want to adopt a donkey," Jess snapped, casting the leaflet aside. "I'm not interested. How can you expect me to be happy about that?"

"Jess, just go and see. They're open on Boxing Day. Give it a chance. Remember it is Christmas and donkeys are part of the nativity scene."

But Jess shook her head and was adamant that she would not go.

Megan looked to her husband for reassurance. Quietly she asked, "Ralph, have we done the right thing? They seemed so nice at the donkey sanctuary when we spoke to them on the phone."

Ralph gave her a hug as he assured her that they had.

Next morning snow had settled on the ground and a feeling of peace hung in the air.

"Jess, come and have some breakfast," Ralph shouted up the stairs and as Megan and he exchanged silent looks, Jess finally appeared and walked slowly into the kitchen.

"We can pop into the sanctuary after breakfast," Megan light-heartedly suggested. "We don't need to stay long. Just time enough for you to be introduced. Will you Jess, please?"

"I don't want to see a smelly donkey!"

But her parents persisted, with Ralph finally coaxing a half-heartedly mumbled okay from her.

Ralph put his arm around Megan as Jess went upstairs to get ready. "Don't worry, love, perhaps the magic of Christmas will come to the rescue."

Megan looked into his face. With a hopeful expression she whispered, "I hope so."

The journey to the donkey sanctuary took about half an hour and Jess seated in the back of the car remained sulky and grumpy.

"Why am I doing this?" Jess moaned to her parents, and Megan feeling her spirit hurt, felt more anxious by the moment.

Ralph gave her a quick wink, and to lighten the mood started singing the Christmas song, *Little Donkey,* much to Jess's annoyance but which made Megan laugh.

Turning down a country lane, Megan could see the buildings of the sanctuary just a little way ahead and in its adjoining fields were the donkeys.

When they arrived at the sanctuary Jess remained

solemnly in the car, while Megan and Ralph went to meet the sanctuary's manager, Alison.

After an informal introduction they felt very much at home, and Alison, happily showed them around.

At last they came back to the field near their car, and Alison pointing to a small donkey in the corner by itself, told them it was desperately in need of a friend.

As much as they tried to coax the donkey to them, it was having none of it, and Megan and Ralph both agreed it reminded them of someone else quite near.

The snow was beginning to fall again, and time was getting on. Jess had remained in the car and by now both Megan and Ralph were beginning to have doubts as they made their way back.

They gave it one last try. Ralph opened the car door and looked at his sullen daughter. "That donkey is as stubborn as you. You would make a good pair."

Astonishingly, Jess seemed to find her dad's comments funny and she burst out laughing. "Okay, okay, I'll go and see it."

"What in those new boots?" Ralph laughingly said.

"Yes, in my new boots," Jess groaned. "But I'm not making any promises, I'm just curious."

Megan and Ralph stayed by the car and watched Jess approach the little donkey. At first it would have nothing to do with her. But both being as stubborn as each other, Jess didn't give up. Finally, after a lot of coaxing and persisting, the little donkey came trotting over to her.

"Well I don't believe it. That's a rascal if ever I saw one," said Megan as she slipped her hand into Ralph's and walked over to where their daughter stood.

Now close to one another they could see that Jess seemed as nervous of the donkey as it was of her, and as the two of them eyed each other up, they tried not to chuckle.

Putting her arm around her daughter, Megan said, "Jess, this is Beth." Then looking at the donkey said, "Beth, this is Jess."

Jess reached out and stroked the donkey gently. It seemed to like the touch and allowed it without moving away. She turned and smiled at her parents. "She's gorgeous!".

Moved by the moment, Megan wiped a tear from her eye and leant closer to Ralph who gave her a hug.

After what seemed like an age, the three of them walked back to the car but not before Jess gave Beth a little wave, and softly said, "See you soon." She glanced at her parents. "I can, can't I?

Megan smiled. "Yes, but you're going to need a new pair of boots."

Jess looked puzzled. "But I've already got some."

"Not fancy, expensive leather boots with heels that are too high. I'm talking about Wellington boots," said Megan and they all laughed.

Ralph wrapped an arm around Megan and Jess, and said, "And who doesn't believe in the magic of Christmas?"

A VERY SPECIAL GIFT

by Ann Evans

A Christmas themed story from Ann.

Last Christmas there had been eight chairs around the dining table, this year there were only six. Maddy had done her best in arranging the chairs so there were no obvious spaces but there had been a tightness in her throat as she'd done so.

But she wouldn't cry, not today, not Christmas Day, a whole eight months since her parents' sudden deaths. She'd done all her grieving.

Today they would all celebrate Christmas as usual. Her, Richard and the kids – and Richard's parents, Nanna Hilda and Grandad Joe. Somehow, she would get through the day.

She'd spent the morning cooking. Amy had helped while Richard took his parents out for a stroll. Tom, being a typical 15-year-old had stayed up in his room, playing one of his new computer games.

Now they were all tucking into turkey, roast potatoes with all the trimmings – and no one had said the words that everyone was thinking. No one wanted to put a downer on what used to be the most festive, wonderful day of the year.

The family complimented Maddy on her cooking, Richard kept the wine glasses topped up. They pulled crackers, wore silly paper hats and groaned at the bad jokes. Still no one said those words. *We miss you. Christmas just isn't the same without you.*

Maddy almost said it, almost said how sad it was without her parents - her children's Granny and Grandpa, but she glimpsed Amy's expression and saw that she was struggling to hold back the tears too. So Maddy swallowed the lump in her throat, took a gulp of wine and almost choked.

The slight commotion was a welcome diversion from the silence that had fallen over everyone. She dabbed her mouth with a napkin and forced herself to smile. Richard caught her eye and she sensed he was feeling guilty because his parents were still here, while hers were gone. Snatched from them in a stupid car accident. She almost said, *it's alright, Richard. Really. I'm alright.* But it wasn't alright. Not really. And she was feeling far from alright.

Past Christmases had been riotous affairs, with laughter and silliness. Today all Maddy could hear was the sound of chewing and the clink of cutlery against china.

Every now and then there would be a burst of conversation, and everyone chipped in with some comment, breaking through the awful deadly awkward silences.

But no one wanted to say what they were all thinking. That they missed them. Richard missed his in-laws; the kids missed their grandparents and Hilda and Joe missed their good friends. But it was as if the subject was taboo. It was Christmas Day, a time of joy, not sorrow.

Only it seemed that everyone was wracked with guilt for continuing with the celebration without her parents. As if what they were doing was disrespectful. But to mention them would reduce everyone to floods of tears and Christmas dinner would be a disaster. And so, the silence went on and on.

Maddy needed to say something. The atmosphere was disastrous as it was. She opened her mouth to speak but Amy got in first.

Her 14-year-old was staring at the Christmas tree in the corner. "There's still an unopened present under the tree."

"Where did that come from?" Maddy mused, not recognising it as anything she'd put there.

Amy nipped across the room to fetch it. "There's no name on it."

"That's not like you pair, to miss a present," Richard remarked, then glanced at his folks. "Is it from you?"

"Not us, dear," said Hilda, helping herself to more sprouts. "You've opened all ours."

"Well someone must recognise it," Maddy puzzled.

The oblong shaped gift was a little bigger than a shoe box and wrapped in gold patterned Christmas paper with a small bow on the top. Amy gave it a little shake. It rattled slightly.

"Tom raised his dark eyebrows. "Well, let's hope it wasn't anything breakable.

Amy wrinkled her nose at her brother. "Well it's obviously not for you. It looks nothing like a computer game."

"Could be a whole collection of games!" he said and grinned hopefully.

"You should be so lucky!"

"Better open it then," Richard suggested, looking intrigued.

Maddy regarded her husband suspiciously. It had to be him. No one else was owning up to it. "You left it there, didn't you, Rich! It's something for sharing. Chocolates?"

He shook his head. "Nope, not me."

"Shall I open it?" Amy asked, then glared at her brother. "If something jumps out at me Tom, you are dead meat!"

He laughed. "Don't look at me!"

Warily, Amy unwrapped the box then made space for it on the table. She lifted the lid at arm's length. "I'm warning you Tom..."

But nothing jumped out. Intrigued they all craned their necks to see what was inside.

There were four individually wrapped items. She opened one of them. "Well this is useful...not! A bottle of brown sauce!"

"Weird!" murmured Tom, carving himself another slice of turkey.

"Why on earth would anyone wrap up a bottle of brown sauce?" Maddy puzzled, glancing at her in-laws.

"Don't look at me," Hilda said with a chuckle. "I'm not going senile *just* yet."

Maddy squeezed her hand and smiled. "Never said you were."

Richard gave a short little laugh. "You know what, that sauce has just reminded me of something." He rubbed his chin. "You'll remember this, Maddy. Remember that first Christmas when you introduced me to your parents?"

"In the Dark Ages," Amy suggested cheekily.

"Stone Age, more like," Tom chipped in.

"Enough of your cheek," Richard warned, still smiling to himself.

"I was seventeen," Maddy recalled immediately. She and Richard had met that autumn, and she'd been so excited at bringing him home to meet her parents.

"There was a party," Richard continued. "And your dad got so sozzled..."

Maddy remembered the evening in all its glory. "And they'd drank every bit of booze in the house, even the cooking sherry..."

"Yes, and so they drank the brown sauce!" Richard said, shaking his head at the memory.

Amy and Tom pulled faces. "Yeuk! That is disgusting" Amy declared but behind the grimace she was laughing.

Nanna Hilda tapped Maddy's hand. "Your parents certainly knew how to throw a party. We've had so much laughter over the years."

"Generous to a fault," Granddad Joe nodded, slurping back his wine.

"Brown sauce," Tom repeated, shaking his head as he fished another item from the box, pulling away the tissue paper. His face lit up immediately. "Oh wow! I remember this."

Maddy looked at what he'd unwrapped. A plastic Christmas fairy in a pink net skirt with sparkly wings, although she looked a bit ancient now. "Goodness me! I thought mum's old Christmas decorations got thrown away when we cleared out the house."

Tom propped the fairy up against the wine bottle. "You can't chuck her away. She's really pretty."

Amy grinned. "Tom! You old softy!"

"Pure nostalgia, this is," Tom remarked, not caring what she thought. "Granny put her on the tree every year, didn't she, Mum?"

Maddy nodded. "Every year. Certainly, from when I was a child... and you Tom... I remember when you were a toddler. You had a real tantrum. You wanted that fairy. You'd been jumping up and down, trying to reach it. Then I turned my back for a moment, and you climbed on the arm of the sofa and launched yourself at it. The whole lot came crashing down."

"You disappeared under a mountain of branches and tinsel," laughed Richard. "Scared us at the time. Then you crawled out with a big smile on your little face clutching that darn fairy."

"So, can I keep it now?" Tom grinned. "It can go on my tree when I get a place of my own. It'll be like a family tradition. I'll pass it down to my kids."

"Planning on getting married then, Tom?" Amy enquired, her eyes twinkling with mischief. "And who in their right mind would want to hitch up with you?"

"They're queuing up," he told her, helping himself to some more roast potatoes.

Maddy added more turkey to her in-law's plates, delighted in the way everyone was eating more heartily now. She turned to her daughter. "Anything else in the box?"

Amy unwrapped the next item. "Ah ha! A ball of wool, a crochet hook and a child's plastic bucket. What *can* it all mean?"

Maddy knew instantly, and she clasped her hands over her mouth.

"I think your mum is remembering something," Granddad Joe remarked, raising his greying eyebrows. "Something you'd rather not talk about, is it, Maddy?"

It was embarrassing, that was for sure. She glanced at Richard, wondering if he'd seen the connection. The pursing of his lips and wiggling eyebrows told her he had.

"Go on, spit it out," Tom groaned.

"Well," began Maddy as the memory came rushing back. "Mum – your granny, was always good at knitting and crocheting. Amy, you remember all the cardigans she made – and Tom, those jumpers?"

Tom's eyes widened. "I remember she made me a jumper with a reindeer on the front that had a red bobble as a nose!"

"Oh yes, that was so cute!" Amy laughed.

Tom shook his head. "It wasn't cute it was embarrassing. I was twelve not two!"

Richard ruffled his son's hair. "You should worry, she made me one with a snowman that had a detachable carrot nose!"

Everybody fell about laughing.

Finally, Amy waggled the plastic bucket. "And what has this to do with knitting? Mum?"

Resigned to share the embarrassing incident, Maddy explained. "Well, before we were married, your dad and I had a few days at the seaside. Mum crocheted me a bikini with metal hoops." She saw her daughter's raised eyebrows. "It was fashionable at the time, trust me."

"I believe you, Mum," laughed Amy.

Maddy continued. "It was a lovely turquoise blue, and your dad and I went paddling in the sea. Well, this big wave caught us, completely drenching us, and... well my bikini was so water-logged and heavy it drooped straight down to my ankles..."

Everyone around the table whooped with laughter.

"Too much information, mother!" Tom exclaimed, head in hands.

"I nearly died of embarrassment!" Maddy groaned, delighted to see her family having so much fun now.

Richard sat there smiling to himself. "Ah! I remember it well..."

Amy dipped into the box again. "Oh, last item."

Maddy got to her feet. "Let's clear away the dishes and bring the pudding in first, shall we?"

Everyone leant a hand, chatting away, recalling all kinds of happy events. There were smiles on faces and the only damp eyes were when someone was laughing too heartily.

Richard poured brandy over the Christmas pudding and put a match to it. It created quite a spectacle, and Maddy recalled the time her dad had done something similar but used too much alcohol and the flames had almost touched the ceiling. Everyone fell about laughing again.

Eventually, Amy opened up the last item. "Okay... a wooden spoon and a slightly bedraggled rose."

Nanna Hilda sniffed the rose. "This is from your own garden. So, whoever wrapped this gift is one of us around the table."

"Course it's one of us," Granddad Joe said. "Although I was beginning to think it was a gift from beyond the grave. It's the sort of fun thing your mam and dad would have thought of doing, Maddy."

She smiled. "Well it's certainly given us a lot of enjoyment, and wonderful memories."

"Y'know what," Tom interrupted. "It's like Granny and Grandpa are actually still around the table with us, having a laugh, reminiscing, like they used to."

"Yes," Maddy breathed, finding that tears were springing into her eyes. Amy rushed over and hugged her. Maddy hugged her back and smiled through her tears

Richard topped everyone's glasses and raised his own. "A toast to absent friends... and relatives. And to everyone we hold dear in our hearts. Happy Christmas everyone and especially to your parents, Maddy."

Everyone echoed his sentiments. "Absent friends and relatives – Merry Christmas!"

Everyone took a drink, and when the glasses had ceased chinking, Amy held up the last two remaining objects, the wooden spoon and the rose. "Okay, so does this jolt any memories? Oh, actually, I think it must be to do with Granny teaching me and Tom how to cook."

Maddy picked up the rose. Hilda was right, it *was* from their garden, although her parents had grown roses too. And then she remembered... "Granny was teaching Amy how to make cakes."

"Which I now do, to perfection!" Amy exclaimed, smiling proudly. Then turned to Nanna Hilda. "Nanna, you have to taste my Christmas cake. I made it this year, didn't I, Mum?"

"You did indeed, and it's fantastic. Granny taught you well," Maddy agreed.

"Anyway, before you'd reached your culinary heights – you were about three at the time. Well, you'd mixed the butter, sugar and eggs, and Granny said, you put the flour in next. Well, you got down from the chair you were standing on to reach the work surface and went off to play... or so we thought."

"Oh no!" Amy groaned. "I remember!"

"What did you do dear?" Nanna Hilda asked.

Maddy explained. "She only went into the garden and picked a whole stack of rose petals and put them all into the cake mix. She'd thought flour was flower!"

Tom fell off his chair laughing.

The rest of the day and the entire evening was devoted to talking about the fun they'd all had over the years, with memories of Granny and Grandpa being at the heart of the conversation.

Eventually everyone made their way up to bed. Maddy caught her daughter's hand as she kissed her goodnight. "It *was* you, wasn't it?" Maddy asked softly.

"What?"

"You know. You put that box of memories under the tree."

Amy drew up her shoulders in an air of innocence. "How could I have known all that stuff? It was all new to me."

Maddy was forced to agree. "Hmm, and Tom wouldn't have known either. Nor Nanna Hilda and Granddad Joe."

"Must have been dad then," Amy shrugged.

Maddy frowned. "It must have been, I suppose.

Although he swears blind that it wasn't."

Amy kissed her cheek. "Perhaps it was Granny and Grandpa after all then. Good night, Mum."

"Goodnight Amy... and happy Christmas."

She crinkled her nose. "Yes, it has been a happy Christmas, hasn't it, Mum?"

"Yes," said Maddy, more at peace than she ever dreamed possible. "A very happy Christmas."

Amy went upstairs into her room. It smelled of roses just as it had done last night. Then over by the window came that same misty flickering of light that she'd seen before. She told herself it was just her imagination – again. Yet it so looked like two people holding hands.

Last night her imagination had conjured up the strangest of thoughts. Suggestions of extra gifts to wrap and place in a box under the tree. A bottle of brown sauce, a wooden spoon and a rose, some blue wool a crochet hook and a child's plastic bucket, and an old Christmas fairy.

Last night she had rubbed her eyes and blinked until the misty light had faded. But the crazy suggestion that she wrap those objects remained. Curious, she'd found what she needed around the house - except for the Christmas fairy, yet that had appeared on the floor behind the long curtains.

So, she'd wrapped everything in colourful tissue paper, covered the box in golden Christmas wrapping, added a bow and slipped it under the tree when no one was looking. Last night it made no sense...

Now Amy gazed at the shimmering glow near her window. It did *so* look like two people holding hands.

And even though she knew it was just her imagination, she blew a kiss and whispered, "Merry Christmas. And thank you."

ONE SILENT NIGHT

by Maxine Burns

The Christmas theme inspired Maxine to write this nostalgic story.

When I was a little girl the arrival of Santa Claus was an unprecedented treat. I lived with Mum and Dad, my two sisters, Elvira and Janine and my brother George, in a small terraced house in Coventry.

We had very little money, but that wasn't unusual in those days. Dad worked as a bank clerk and Mum was a part time cleaner. I didn't even know that Mum worked until I was quite grown up, as she started her job very early and was home before we children were even out of our beds.

Although we were poor, we ate well. Mum cooked lovely food: shepherd's pie, sausage and mash, tasty stews and she baked the most wonderful fruit cakes. Our milk was delivered in jugs, and the coal arrived on the back of a horse-drawn cart, driven by a man blackened from head to foot in coal dust. Judged by today's standards, we didn't have much, but we were very happy.

Christmas was wonderful in those days. Very special. It didn't start with cards and gifts in the shops in October, like it does now. No. Christmas Eve was when it all happened. At least for us children.

No doubt Mum had been saving all year, so that we could all have something each of us wanted very badly. One year I had a golden-haired doll. I called her Alice. She had blue eyes and pink smiley lips and Mum knitted some beautiful clothes for her. I can smell that sweet rubbery scent now, if I concentrate.

We would hang our stockings along the mantelpiece.

Dad would let the fire go out so that Santa could come down the chimney safely.

Elvira and I would put a couple of mince pies, baked that morning with help from Mum, onto a plate. Janine and George would carefully pour a small glass of sherry. These were for Santa. Next we would pop a peeled carrot on the hearth for Rudolph. Then to bed.

Me, Elvira and Janine shared a room and George slept in a small bed in Mum and Dad's room. We girls felt really sorry for him as he had to lie still and be very quiet, so as not to disturb our parents. We, in our own room, could talk and giggle, lie awake and listen for the tinkle of the bells that would herald Santa's arrival. I swear I heard them every year, just as I drifted into sleep.

Morning would arrive and although it was very early and dark, we would leap out of bed with uncharacteristic energy. If we were lucky, snow had fallen in the night and I would run down, open the back door and study the ground for reindeer tracks. Mostly the snow was thick and they had been covered.

Dad would light the fire whilst Mum made a cup of tea and put the bacon on to sizzle gently as we opened our present and looked in our stockings, each in turn. Everyone would 'oo' and 'ah' at the nuts, the little sweet oranges and the chocolate coins, wrapped in gold paper. These, we were allowed to eat before breakfast. They tasted all the better for that!

George had a fort one year, and another Elvira had a doll house. We hardly saw her for a month, she was so engrossed with it.

Then, Mum would cook the dinner. A chicken, all the trimmings. Crackers and pop. A sherry for Mum and a bottle of cold stout for Dad, a treat that had been cooling in the yard, under the snow, all morning. Dad always carried the Christmas pudding in, alight with holly on top, the red berries sparkling in the boozy flames.

I wish I had a photograph to show you. I can remember every precious minute, all their faces, lit up with happiness on a perfect day.

We children would then wrap up, coats, hats, scarves and gloves and go into the garden to play. We loved a snow fight. Other children would be out too, some on their Christmas bikes, and we would all go through the entry, out into the yard to share what we'd had and snowball each other.

Later we would do a puzzle, although I preferred to read a book. Dad always managed to get me a new one and I would sit on the floor in front of the fire and read until tea.

Tea-time! What a treat that was. Mum would fry up the left-over dinner, and we all fought over the crispy pieces of potato and sprouts and stuffing. Then Mum's *piece de resistance*. The trifle. Sponge and sweet tinned fruit with custard. Definitely no jelly. Snowy white thick cream topped with grated chocolate. Mmm. Lovely.

Bedtime came all too soon. We would grumble and sulk for a bit, but eventually we'd trudge upstairs, yawning in spite of ourselves. We would clamber into bed, heavy eyed, replete, content and be asleep in a flash, after a wonderful day.

That was all a very long time ago. Mum and Dad are long gone. Poor George was killed in the war. His ship went down, torpedoed by the Germans, mid Atlantic. I try not to think about it anymore. For years I would hear him crying in that cold, black sea, as he slowly drowned.

Janine married and had a son, Peter. I was once engaged to be married, but he was shot down over Berlin and his body never recovered. That dreadful war.

Well, that was it for me. I continued to live in the family home with Elvira. I worked as a secretary for the Lord Mayor and got Elvira a job in the canteen. She was never the same after Freddie jilted her and she occasionally spent time in the asylum at Warwick.

Even so, we had some good Christmases. I never lost my love of the season, so we always made it special. We had a Christmas cruise one year and Santa still managed to find us, right in the middle of the Med! Another time we helped to cook and serve the festive meal in a hostel for the homeless. That was a good day. So many people, some of them so young too, with no-one to care for them. Santa had his job cut out that year but, as usual, he came up trumps. It was lovely to see all those pinched, thin faces light up with pleasure.

Elvira died one Christmas Eve, so that year Christmas passed in misery and sadness. It was the only grim Christmas I've had. I lay sleepless, as usual, but instead of joy and anticipations, I felt only heartache and apprehension. My lovely sister gone. The last of my family.

Janine's son Peter is a good lad and has a very nice wife. For the last couple of years, they have insisted I spend the day with them. I don't mean to be ungrateful, but they have two teenage children. They have their own life. They mean well, but I don't really enjoy being there. It's cold, I can't hear the television and they have their Christmas meal so late – 5 o'clock last year. And they don't really notice me. They see an old lady sitting in the corner, who needs to be helped upstairs to the toilet and needs her turkey cut up, and who can't eat a lot anyway. They all chat and laugh at the jokes in the crackers – just as we did all those years ago, but it's not the same and it makes me sad.

I don't know if I can do it again, but I don't know how to refuse and I feel so ungrateful, but I would rather be on my own, live the day through my memories and as you can see I have so many good ones.

They are coming to pick me up in the morning, Christmas Day.

It is Christmas Eve. I wrap a present to myself and pour glasses of sherry. One for me and one for Santa. I put a mince pie on a plate and leave a peeled carrot for Rudolph, then I go up to bed to lie sleepless. Even after all these years, I can feel butterflies fluttering in my tummy as I wait. I start to doze then sit up as I hear the bells that herald Santa. How loud they are!

I watch as the bedroom door opens and there he is. He is plump and round with a jolly face, a long luxurious white beard, just as you'd expect. Only this year he leaves nothing. Instead he takes my hand and in an instant, I am on the sleigh. There is Dancer and Prancer. And Oh, here is Rudolph, my favourite. He turns to look at me, nods his beautiful head and I smile at him, reach out to touch his back.

Then we are flying through the sky, looking down on the world. It is so bright and white, and I wave goodbye.

We are home. My house has a log fire and is warm and cosy. Better yet, Mum, Dad, Elvira, Janine and our little George live here too. We have no television and we talk to each other. All my aches and pains are gone.

I know now that Santa isn't just one man. When you think about it, how could he be? There are many Santa's. People who have kept faith with Santa all their lives, who listened each Christmas Eve for the bells, left Santa a drink and Rudolph a carrot. People like me.

Santa takes us and we have Christmas forever.

A LOWLY CONVENIENCE STORE

By Bec Woods

On the theme of Christmas, Bec was inspired by the corner shop that's always open, even on Christmas morning.

Countryfile had promised a frost on Christmas morning and sure enough as Janice got to the store, it was crisp and white and even.

The Supermoon that had peaked at 6.11 had gone to bed; where I should be, thought Janice as she raised the steel shutter.

Inside the shop it was dark and cold and though the strip lighting burst into life Janice could still see her breath. Bet he's switched the heating off, she thought as she made her way to the kitchenette at the back of the store.

"Hello!" called a voice over the sound of the kettle. Janice peered around the doorway and saw a dishevelled man at the store entrance, casting his eyes up and down the rows of merchandise but not seeming to see anything.

"Got any pickled cabbage?" he asked, a smirk creasing the two days' growth on his cheeks.

Janice frowned and joined him in looking aimlessly up and down the shelves. Strange thing to have on a Christmas dinner she thought spying the pickled onions and heading towards them.

"Oh, yes we do," she said with surprise as a jar caught her eye.

"And some ice-cream too?" The man pulled his coat around what appeared to be a pyjama shirt.

Poor thing thought Janice, he's been dragged out of bed to get the shopping. She smiled at him and went towards a frozen cabinet.

"Due any day now," he said as they went back towards the till. "Be glad when it arrives so we can get back to normal."

He handed over a note as crumpled as he was, then scooping up his goods, wished Janice a Happy Christmas and left.

Janice didn't hear the next person come in as she was busy discounting the frozen turkeys. She did sense the cold, hard stare though, and looking up saw a small, bundle of wool and tweed, supported by a wheeled shopping trolley.

"Where are the papers?" the woman called to her.

Janice walked towards her, "The magazines..."

"Not the magazines, the papers." The woman's eyes were like jet beads and her mouth like screwed up tissue paper.

Janice gestured to the dog-eared remains of yesterday's papers, which languished below the rows of magazines.

The woman moved forward ramming her trolley into Janice's ankles. Wincing Janice got a whiff of mothballs and muscle rub.

"They're yesterdays. I want today's," said the woman loud and slow.

"There aren't any today," said Janice hoping that the woman would take her custom elsewhere. Thankfully, the woman shared this sentiment and grumbling obscenities, she pin-balled herself and her trolley off the fixtures to the door.

Janice glanced at the clock. Nearly nine. Wonder if I might risk a slice of toast without setting the smoke alarm off but hey at least I can warm my hands over the elements.

Sated by another cup of tea and toast she began

unpacking boxes of wines and spirits. At least these won't give me any grief she thought. Suddenly she spied movement out of the corner of her eye and saw a hooded figure swaying to and fro by the shop door.

Not one of the local drunks, today of all days, she thought as she went to open the door.

She hadn't reached the door before it opened and the figure had scooped back its hood to reveal the spotty face of a teenage boy.

"You open?"

Janice blinked and when she realised it was a genuine question waved at the shelves of goods.

"Got any potatoes?" The boy continued to look at her, feet firmly rooted to the spot.

Janice thought about asking what type and how many but instead just went to the trays where the vegetables were kept. Shifting peppers and parsnips she was soon holding aloft a small bag of Jersey Royals.

"These do?" she asked knowing she wouldn't get an answer. "I've just reduced them, so you've got a bargain."

The boy raised his eyebrows and then dropped a fiver on the counter.

As she counted out his change the boy seemed to come to life. "Got any discounted boxes of chocolates?" he asked looking directly at the shelf laden down with confectionery.

"Just about to do it," said Janice snatching up her pricing gun. Merrily she twisted the knobs on the old-fashioned device and stamped one of the largest boxes with the exact price of the boy's change. Oh well I'll blame it on the cold she thought if her boss queried it later.

"These for your Mum?" she asked as she closed the till and handed the chocolates to the youth.

"No, they're for me," he said opening the shop door. "Merry Christmas."

Janice watched him slip and slide over the frosty ground and hoped her next customer had more Christmas spirit.

The hours passed and no-one else came. A few cars slowed as if the drivers were thinking about things forgotten, but then accelerated away. The superstores would be open tomorrow.

Yes, why bother, thought Janice as she pulled down the shutter and shunted the padlock in place. It's just another day.

And like any other day she headed home to her cold and empty flat.

OUT WITH THE OLD

By Marilyn Pemberton

A bit of Christmassy flash fiction from Marilyn.

The tree decorations are back in the loft. Now, what the hell shall I do with the presents? They are still in "his" and "her" piles, the "hers" far taller than the "his", as always. I know what she has got me - a quick feel on Christmas Eve had confirmed socks, underwear and a funny Christmas jumper. I might as well open them, you can't have too many socks and underwear, after all. I know what is in hers, of course, and I throw them unopened into the bin. Don't worry, there is nothing of value - in fact, in most cases there is nothing in them at all apart from screwed up pieces of newspaper and the odd tin.

Oh, I never said. The body was the thing I disposed of first, naturally.

RETAIL THERAPY

by Bec Woods

Christmas Eve at a large shopping store – fun, yes? Bec saw it more like this...

The bear costume she was wearing was making Katie sweat beneath the shop lights. For seven hours she'd tried to persuade Hancock customers that they needed Hancock Harry, a smaller version of her suited self, yet stuffed with wading, for the bargain price of £10.77, with seventy-seven pence from every bear sold going to charity.

After the initial flurry of interest when the shop opened at 8 am, the only people to touch a teddy was Katie, her manager, who liked to rearrange the display, and a small child with sticky fingers who succeeded in matting the fur with red gloop. By the look in the child's eye Katie had thought that the girl was just looking to clean her hands rather than pet the bear as she released it easily when Katie tried to persuade the mother to buy it.

Now approaching six o'clock Katie had the prospect of the first wave of drunks from the pub next door, suddenly remembering it was Christmas Eve and the need to buy an ever-expanding list of presents before the shop closed at six.

In fact, the first of them was nearing the desk, gently bobbing like a pinball between rails of clothes whilst singing the first two lines of Jingle Bells over and over again. Spying Katie, the drunk dramatically stopped dead, reared back on his heels before tipping forward, finger wagging.

"Hey, Mr. Bear, where's the potatoes?"

Katie, now used to the barrier of her disguise, looked at the glassy eyes that rolled like lottery balls waiting to be plucked into focus, and drew in the scent of eau de ale.

"Po-tay-toes!" the drunk spread wide his arms and threw his head back. Shoppers skirted the inebriated redeemer and Katie felt trapped by duty to remain at her post.

"Little bears," the drunk now leered at the toy bears, "p'raps, you can tell me."

Katie thought she saw them shrink back and tried not to laugh as one toppled off the table.

"I'll save you," called the drunk, diving to the floor then rolling about with laughter at his predicament.

"Okay, Sir," came the voice of Al, Hancock's security guard, a burly man who worked nights in the local sandwich factory.

Katie felt relieved and shivering, realised that the cold sweat on her skin had little to do with the unforgiving artificial fibres of her outfit. As she adjusted her head to let some fresh air in, she spied Agatha near the table of tree decorations. She watched as the older woman held-up a bauble and then dropped it into her shopping bag. A nearby shopper nudged her husband as Agatha repeated this action several times before moving onto a stand of earrings.

"She's like a magpie," Al had said the first time Katie had seen it happen and had called him over.

"But why don't you prosecute her?" Katie had asked as Agatha had toddled to the door under Al's watchful gaze.

"Coz, she's not well. It's something in her head. Been like it for years, ever since I've been here. Her husband lost his job. Mind you he's got a new one now – bringing back everything that she's not got a receipt for.

Sometimes we even get stuff that she hasn't lifted from here, or stuff that she had occasionally remembered to pay for."

Looking at her now, Katie wondered if she could persuade Agatha to take a bear, just so other folk might get interested.

There'd been one offer to purchase a bear by Loopy Lucy, the bag lady who came into the shop for a warm when the library was closed. But Katie had to say that Hancock's didn't accept IOUs and that anyway the cuddly toy was too small for a pillow and released toxic gases if you threw it on a brazier.

Katie shifted her weight and pressed two paws into the flesh either side of her spine. She wished that there was a ledge or pillar that she could lean against, but every available space was crammed with merchandise.

The table that the bears were piled up on was an old paste table that had been found in the display cubbyhole and she'd already found out how unstable it was when she'd pressed down on it to write out a price card. Fortunately, there'd only been a few bears displayed at the time, though it was the devil's own job trying to rescue them from a mob of gobby teenagers who'd picked the bears up and threw them over Katie's head as she went to retrieve them.

"What you doing later?" Trish from budget fragrances asked as she returned from her afternoon tea break.

"Crashing out in front of the telly with a big glass of egg-nog and my selection box." Katie sighed in anticipation of the prospect.

"My Nan used to drink egg-nog," said Trish checking her make-up in a mirrored shop fitting. "Used to scoop the last bit out of the glass with her little pinkie." She wiggled her little finger at Katie before clip clopping back to her sentry point, with stool, in front of row upon row of cut-price scent. "Smells like disinfectant, but if you put a bow on it, call it a fancy name and sell it at a bargain price, people buy it by the gallon." She'd said of her products.

As the tannoy announcer cheerfully proclaimed that the store would be closing in five minutes, the mood lifted amongst the staff. And with a final push they tried to inject the final strains of Christmas goodwill and joy into their service to customers.

That looks lovely on you madam, Why not take two, there's always someone you've forgotten to buy for and *I'm sure it'll come in useful,* was the reckless encouragement of assistants to whom the misery of processing returns on Boxing Day was like a vision of Christmas future - difficult to anticipate.

Al began singing along to the piped carols that had been playing on a loop since the town's Christmas lights had been switched on the weekend after Bonfire Night. Even Katie hummed along as she prepared the sale tags that would garrotte the bears in two days' time.

As she surreptitiously tried to fill out her sales sheet, she became aware of someone close to the desk. Looking up she saw a young woman in her twenties, eyes shining with unshed tears as she handled one of the bears.

"My mum bought me one of these when I was a kid," she said, her voice thick with emotion.

Katie smiled from beneath her costume and then realising it'd be of no comfort to the women made an exaggerated display of opening her arms and then clasping her hands together.

"Maybe she's got you another one this year," said Katie wondering if any of the sales over the previous week had been to anyone other than a member of staff's family.

"Doubt it," said the woman replacing the bear.

"Well no saying you can't buy yourself one – and get her one too." Katie picked up two bears and offered them up like orphans seeking a home.

"She's not about for me to give it to her."

"You could save..." Katie extended her arms a fraction.

"She died earlier this month."

There was silence as the woman looked at Katie and for once Katie felt that the outfit was no barrier to the embarrassment she felt. She dropped the two quarries back on the table.

"I'm..." she began to say as the tannoy cut in: 'Please note that the store is now closed. We'd like to thank you for your custom and wish you a safe journey home. Good night and Merry Christmas' followed by giggling and a deep Ho! Ho! Ho.

The woman had moved off and was now being corralled with other customers out of the door by Al. When the last of them left he came over to Katie who was slowly removing the head of her costume.

"Well that's another Christmas done and dusted," he said.

"Yes," said Katie, "I'm glad it's only once a year."

THE KINGFISHER

By Catherine Wilson

This morning we are doing long division.
Yesterday was for freedom.
Long division is for today.

Yesterday's kingfisher is for tomorrow.
Long division will not wait.
Brilliant feathers gleaming in sunlight.
He darted; swooped for a fish.
A shining writhing minnow; tiny.
Tiny, without a chance.

My pencil is short, broken; chewed.
Sunbeams stream through high narrow windows,
Where feathered tree-tops waver.
Why are they so high?

When did we do short division, Miss?
Sharpen pencils for today's long division.
Wrong means rapped fingers.

Yesterday's brook rippled like warm silk across my fingers.
He is out there swooping and diving.
Whilst long division is what we are doing in here today.
When did we do short division, Miss?

Brown classroom; awash with ink stained desks.
Scabbed knees tucked, doing long division, as
Bird sounds pour through high narrow windows.
Why are they so high?

Sunbeams sprinkled yesterday's brook with magic.
Eyes are down for long division today.
Shouldn't short division come first, Miss?

Birdsong streams through high narrow windows.
Why are they so high?
Today we are doing long – very long division.

BUSINESS OR PLEASURE, MISS?

By Alex Bartlett

A class exercise incorporating a colour, a weather condition and a way of moving.

Stephanie sighed, the 100 metres from the tube station to the Reception looked a mile away with the rain pouring down. She pulled her coat over her blonde hair, let out another long sigh then ran as fast as her purple heels would let her. She stumbled through the Reception door, nearly breaking her ankle as she skidded on the marble floor.

"Be careful," came a soft cry from in front of her.

She didn't need to look to know who's voice it was. She steadied herself and smiled at Tom, the tall, dark receptionist.

"I'm fine thanks, Tom,' she assured him as water dripped from her soaked coat. "We can always rely on the British weather."

"Let me take that soaking coat, Miss.' His arm was already reaching out and touching her sleeve.

Although it wasn't skin contact, she felt her heart quicken and goose bumps appeared on her arms. Tom had only been with the firm a few months, but her attraction to him had grown stronger over that time. He had been such a gentleman from the start, completely different from the other guys she had to deal with.

"Thank you," she blushed, letting him remove the coat, whilst wishing he could remove other items of her clothing too.

"You're welcome, Miss," he responded, completely unaware of her reaction. "You've got time to dry off before the 9am meeting."

"Yes, of course," she said with a sigh.

Pleasure would have to wait. Business was currently the priority.

BEWARE INNOCENT LOOKING LITTLE OLD LADIES

By Ella Cook

The theme of a garden got Ella thinking.

"I don't believe it. They got them all." Mabel's voice croaked painfully as she looked around her previously picture-perfect garden. "There isn't a single one left. The little buggers got them all."

"I'm so sorry." Lily rested her hand on her friend's shoulder, before rummaging through her bag for a tissue. "Here you go." She bent down to pick something up from the grass.

"Thanks." Mabel sniffed gratefully before snorting into the tissue. "It's just so horrible. First it was Libby's, then old Mrs. Smith's up the road..."

"Don't forget the memorial garden."

"How could I?" Mabel stared around her empty garden miserably. "And now mine. They've had every single one of them. Not a single pointed hat or fishing rod anywhere to be seen."

"I know." Lily commiserated, while hoping that she'd firmly locked her back gate. "Let's get you inside and get you a nice cup of tea. Then we can call the sheriff and tell him the gnome nappers have struck again."

"There's no point," Mabel wailed as she handed over her keys. "That overstuffed shirt couldn't lead a successful investigation out of a wet paper bag."

"I'd love to argue with you, but I can't. I remember when little Stevie Tucker went missing from the fayre."

"...and the Sheriff had launched a borough-wide search and called the state troopers before remembering he'd put him in the back of his squad car as punishment for putting superglue in the clowns' red noses. I remember." Lily stifled a laugh. "It took poor Mr Crocker three days to get all the sponge bits out of his moustache. And his poor nose really was red."

Mabel passed her friend the milk and reached for the cake tin. After such a terrible shock she felt like she deserved a treat. But as she pulled it out of the cupboard, her eyes were drawn towards the window, and she sighed sadly. "My whole garden looks so bare without all my little fairies and gnomes. And the little buggers trampled my begonias too!"

"I'll help you replant them tomorrow." Lily offered.

"Thank you. But that's not the point." Mabel glared at the desolate wasteland of her former fairy garden, and at the now empty toadstool ring. "They shouldn't be allowed to get away with this. If only we knew who was behind it."

Lily patted her pocket thoughtfully. "What would you do? If you knew who it was, I mean."

"I'd teach them a bloody lesson. Nasty little gnome nappers. My grandchildren bought me some of those, you know. They'll be so upset when they find out they're missing."

"Speaking of grandchildren, I should get going to pick mine up." She gave Mabel a reassuring hug. "Try not to get too upset by it all."

"Thanks." Mabel nodded morosely and stared out of the window.

As Lily made her way past the fairy-less wishing well, she drew a single key out of her pocket and peered at the personalised keyring – S.T. She knew exactly who that belonged too. She rummaged in her bag and produced her multi-tool penknife and smiled to herself.

The next morning, little Stevie Tucker raced out of his house, his backpack empty and his mind filled with mischief. He leaped onto his beloved red BMX and shot out of his driveway.

But before he'd gotten to the end of the road, the bike rattled to a halt. Confused, he jumped off and stared in amazement at his tyres – both had been let down, and his chain no longer seemed to fit. Grumbling to himself, he dragged the bike home, cursing his bad luck.

And the fairy garden? Well the next morning it was back exactly as it was – almost as if by magic.

WAITING

by Marilyn Pemberton

The ocean inspired this powerful piece of flash fiction from Marilyn

Maria stood motionless at the water's edge, oblivious to the wave that foamed over her feet, soaking her dress almost up to her waist. She could not, would not, believe that her Thomas was gone. He had no right to leave her, not now she was with child, and she felt a surge of primeval anger well up inside her and she screamed into the storm, "Thomas!"

People came and tried to get her to go home but she knew, and the child deep in her womb knew, that if she did not lose hope then the wait would not be in vain. So, she scanned the horizon continuously, almost wishing a boat into existence, so much so that when a red dot appeared in the distance and grew ever bigger, she was not sure whether it was in her imagination. It was only when she heard a voice, just discernible over the scream of the wind, "Maria!" that she knew her child would not grow up fatherless.

FOOD

by Marilyn Pemberton

This class exercise had a foodie theme and inspired Marilyn to write this.

The sound of the sizzling fat and the smell of the cooked meat made me salivate and I actually licked my lips. I waited for the fatty bits to brown and crisp then turned the strips over. Wagner was playing in the background; he always induced a good appetite. I chose blackcurrant tea this morning; I liked the slightly bitter taste and the way it cleansed the palate.

It was ready!

I used a spatula to transfer the strips onto a large white porcelain plate, the one with the real gold border – my best service. I arranged them into five equidistant parallel lines. There were no other garnishments; I wanted nothing to detract from the experience. I put the plate reverently onto the pristine, white tablecloth, tucked a starched white napkin into my collar, picked up my solid silver knife and fork, made a cut and took my first mouthful. The taste was sublime, almost orgasmic.

Thank you, Peter; I look forward to eating more of you.

PHOENIX

by Bec Woods

The theme of class exercise 'Smile' prompted Bec to create this piece of flash fiction.

He smiled as he loaded the crumpled paper onto the flames. It was engulfed with the same fervour that it had been hoarded.

A small sense of victory lubricated his stoking of the fire. It had taken many, many months to persuade Lily to part with the padding that insulated her life against reality. It had only been a chance viewing of a television programme on hoarding that had embarrassed her into thinking that she may have a similar problem.

Through his laughter Phil had tried to soften the prospect of trawling through years of memories. Memories that were stitched into Lily's soul.

Even though the audit of her life started slowly it soon gathered momentum and Phil could hardly keep up with the steady stream of notes and jottings, memos and memoirs that were becoming the combustible compost of his wife's life.

After the initial stock of fuel had been piled into the old metal dustbin, and the flames were working their way through the kindle, Phil stopped to read a missive. Uncrumpling the paper he smiled at the date on the top of the sheet – two days before he and Lily had gone on their first date. Beneath was written "Agreed to go on date with Sam's mate – see how it goes." Phil frowned as he tried to think who Sam might be.

THE MOST BEAUTIFUL SMILE

By Marilyn Pemberton

The 'smile' theme prompted Marilyn to share an extract from her novel, The Jewel Garden.

He gave me the most beautiful smile I ever saw. He can't have been more than five-years-old and Khalim, our house boy, had grabbed the young urchin as he tried to run off with my purse. He wore just a tattered pair of grubby, once-white shorts, his feet were dusty and calloused, his skinny brown legs were slightly bowed, and his knees were as scabby as only a young boy's can be. He had black, black hair, unwashed and unruly, and black, black eyes that sparkled in the strong sunlight. And rather than looking abashed and guilty he just gave me a gappy, winning smile, the most beautiful smile I ever saw. Until I gave him a few coins out of my purse, and his smile became broader and even more beautiful.

NO LAUGHING MATTER

By Bec Woods

The David Bowie song 'The Laughing Gnome' may have been Bec's inspiration for this story.

Conrad couldn't help but smile at the little fella. And the little fella couldn't help but smile at Conrad. They were still smiling at each other when Garry came into the room.

"What you doin', you muppet?" Garry asked.

"I can't help smiling. It's infectious," Conrad said, looking at the garden gnome, a brightly painted figure with cheeks as red as its hat.

"Creepy if you ask me," Garry said going over to a holdall on the table and examining their cache of stolen laptops, mobiles and jewellery. "Just as well we were able to bust into the neighbour's house."

"I'm going to keep him," Conrad said.

Garry left the holdall and snatched the figure from Conrad, tipping it this way and that, examining its provenance.

"We might be able to get something for it." Suddenly, he called out, dropped the figure and rubbed his hand. "The little bugger just bit me."

"Who's the muppet now?" asked Conrad replacing the smiling gnome on the table. "It must have been a garden spider that bit you."

After they'd offloaded the other stolen goods they sat back with a beer. One beer became two which became three and shortly they had a crate full of empty bottles and an urge to eat takeaway.

"What do you fancy, Chinese, Indian or good old fish and chips?" Conrad swayed like the living room floor was the deck of a ship.

"Not bothered. What do you want?" Garry loomed close to the gnome's face, laughing a beery breath over it.

Conrad blinked as he thought he saw the gnome wrinkle its nose. "Hey, it's just shrunk back from your bad breath."

"How much you had to drink?" Garry staggered to his feet.

"Same as you." Conrad reared up and swayed across the room. As he closed the door behind him, he heard Garry say, "I don't know what you're laughing at."

Twenty minutes later and weighed down with chicken chow mein, Conrad came back to find Garry lying on the sofa the gnome clutched to his chest. As he unpacked the meal his friend roused, looking perplexed to find himself hugging the gnome.

"Where've you been? I'm starving."

"I had to pick up something for Geronimo." Conrad went back out into the hallway.

"Who's Geronimo?" Garry asked the bearded gnome.

Conrad came in with another gnome. Perhaps younger than the first as his nose was less red, and his belly less rounded.

"Meet Malcolm," Conrad placed the second gnome next to the first.

"Malcolm?"

"Yes. Malcolm and Geronimo," said Conrad pointing at one gnome then the other.

"What are we going to do with them?"

"Keep them. They make me smile. Come on let's eat before it gets cold."

As Conrad shovelled chow mein and fried rice into his mouth he eyed the two gnomes. When he reached for a prawn cracker, he was sure he saw movement out of the corner of his eye. Quickly he turned but all he saw were two gnomes smiling back at him.

"We haven't even got a garden," Garry said later as he turned the lights off in the sitting room.

"They're home gnomes," said Conrad laughing. "Anyway, we don't want some scumbag trying to nick them, do we?"

As he lay in his bed that night going over the evening's events, Conrad began to laugh. First it was just a quick exhale of breath, then it was a chuckle which became longer and deeper with every caught breath. Before long he was sitting up in bed clutching his sides trying to contain his merriment.

A bang on the wall distracted him momentarily; he must have woken Garry with the noise. He rolled out of bed, still laughing. As he pushed the door to his friend's room his breath caught as he saw the two gnomes clasping their tiny hands over his friend's mouth and nose.

Garry's arms were flailing, trying to swat the figures away, but they clung like limpets to his airways, smiling benignly at each other. Conrad stared and began to laugh and laugh, gulping for air.

All those that heard the laughter, through the paper-thin walls of the flat, smiled too. It was nice to hear people enjoying themselves. It made a change from the misery and depravity that usually pervaded the tower block.

When news of the post-mortem came through, people were not surprised to discover the two men had died of asphyxiation. They were into all sorts one, of the neighbours said.

Geronimo and Malcolm were soon returned to their rightful owner, Miss Prist, an octogenarian who lived in the well-heeled suburb that butted up to the tower block.

"Boys, boys," she said as she took the gnomes from the policeman and went to place them in the garden by the small pond. "What have you been up to?"

"We recovered them from the flat of two petty criminals," PC Wishaw said. "We would have pressed charges, but the men died before we had chance. Really strange, they both had these silly grins on their faces when we found the bodies."

"Yes, it's no laughing matter," Miss Prist said smiling as she patted the cheeks of her two little gnomes. "No laughing matter at all."

THE BIG GUNS

By Margaret Mather

A local bookshop inspired Margaret to write this story

The closed sign dangles from the bookshop window but I'm not alone. The staff have stayed behind and I am curious to know why. Floating nearer to the table I hover, waiting for the discussion to begin.

"Whose stupid idea was it to have a bonding session?" asks Daffy, the Saturday girl.

"I suggested it," Charlie, the owner, pipes up. "Do us all good to share experiences and life stories," he turns to look at Emm, his wife. Blushing, she fiddles with the pearls around her slender neck and smiles back at her adoring husband.

"All right by me," says Charlie's brother, Art, seizing the opportunity to be close to Daffy.

"I have a cat at home, she'll be wondering where I am," interrupts Mary.

Bless her, good, kind Mary. She helps out every day, dressed in the same old tweed skirt and cream coloured, high-neck blouse.

In silence, I watch as they straighten books, fidget with chairs, drum impatient fingers on the table and gaze out of the bullion windows at the dark, deserted, cobbled streets.

The bookshop, my home, had changed a great deal since I'd first inhabited it. No more human waste falling on your head from an upstairs window now and candles are only used for decorative purposes. Pity, I do miss a flickering flame, so much more atmospheric.

"I've had enough of this," Daffy moans. "Let's do something exciting. I know we'll hold a séance."

"What, hold a what, a séance? NOOOOO," I scream, horrified by the word. "That's asking for trouble. I'm the resident ghost and I don't want anyone else stealing my turf or worse, sharing my space."

They can't hear me.

I have to stop them.

Whirling around the room, I send books flying from shelves. That should scare them.

"Windy out tonight, gets in every crack and crevice," says Mary, picking them up and popping them back. Returning to her seat, she carries on, along with the others, cutting out the alphabet from scraps of coloured paper.

Gliding over to a chair, I lift it up and send it crashing to the floor.

"Wobbly leg," says Art, picking it up and wedging it underneath a table.

What do I have to do to save these fools? They are heading towards dangerous territory. I switch the kettle on hoping to spook them, but Charlie puts it down to an electrical fault. Idiots, they have no idea what they are about to unleash.

Scarcely able to look, I hold a cushion to my face. Peering over it I see Daffy arrange the letters in a circle.

"I've seen my mum do this," she says. "Everyone puts a finger on the glass, we ask questions and the glass spells out the answers. No pushing mind, we'll know if someone's messing around."

They all giggle, apart from Mary. Strange one, Mary, can't seem to figure her out.

"Ok, are we ready?" Mumbled approval follows. "Right then, fingers on glass."

They all duly oblige. And in a shaky voice, nothing like her own, I listen as Daffy whispers, "Hello, is there anybody there?"

The glass moves slowly around the table spelling out the word, Y-E-S.

Furious, I try once more to dissuade them. Grabbing hold of the table with both hands I desperately try to overturn it but it's too heavy. The weight of five people keep it anchored to the floor.

"Who's moving it?" demands Art, who thinks of himself as a bit of an amateur sleuth.

All the others pipe up, "Not me."

"Well someone is," he says.

"Oh, shut up, Art," Daffy replies carrying on in that irritating voice. "Who is it?"

The glass spells out, M-A -R-Y then pauses before spelling out S-H-E-L-L-Y.

"Oh, my, how exciting," gushes Emm. Charlie pats her hand affectionately.

I, on the other hand am doubtful. Mary Shelly, a likely story. I try to remove the glass, but it sticks to the table.

Without warning, Charlie, Emm, Art and Daffy stand up knocking over their chairs. With eyes wide and staring, mouths clamped shut, bodies rigid, they are unable to move.

I knew this would happen. They've been possessed but by whom, I wonder?

Mary, still seated, turns to look at me with a face full of venom, then hisses, "And you, Edgar Allan Poo, how dare you steal my home all those years ago, forcing me to live a cold miserable existence in the outdoor toilet. Well not anymore. This was my home before you turned up. I'd only popped out for an hour and when I came back, you'd taken over my spot. I've waited years to return to my rightful place. You know the rules, one home, one ghost."

Flabbergasted, I retort, "It's Poe not Poo, you ignorant woman. And I watched you pick those books up and cut out letters. How can you possibly be a ghost?"

"It was an apparition you saw, nobody else knows I'm here."

"How have you managed to keep it from me all these years?"

"It wasn't difficult, you're not very bright."

"Bright enough to write a physiological thriller, you just wrote about some stupid monster."

"I sold more books than you, Poo."

"No, you didn't and stop calling me, Poo."

"Yes, I did."

"No, you didn't."

"I bloody well..."

"Shut up both of you." Words tumble out of Charlie's mouth but it's not his voice. "I've sold more than you two put together. Oliver Twist, A Christmas Carol, A Tale of Two Cities, popular then and still popular today."

"Is that you, Dickens?" I ask. "Is it really you, my old friend?"

"Of course, it's me."

"A Tale of Two Cities? Never heard of that one."

"That's because you were dead when it was first published."

"Oh, that explains it then."

"Did I just hear you picking on the lovely Mary? I knew you'd moved in, but I didn't know that Mary had lived here first. Kick her out, did you?" he asks, pointing his cane at me.

"No, I didn't kick her out. The place was empty when I turned up. No ghosts of any kind. Where do you haunt these days, Charlie boy?

"Here and there, but mostly Portsmouth where I was born. The house is fine, but in the summer, lots of people tramp in and out wanting to know where I slept, what I ate, where my parents slept. The truth is, I only lived there for six months but the local folks running it have a living to make I suppose. Puts me off a bit. Wouldn't mind living here for the summer months." Lighting his pipe, he lies back in the chair and puts his feet up on the table.

"Well that's not going to happen," I snap.

"Over my dead body," says Mary.

"But you are dead, Mary," Dickens points out.

"Oh yes, so I am, still, I want you and, Pooy here, out of my home immediately."

"He's going nowhere!" The words burst forth from Emm's mouth.

The three of us, startled, look at each other and then at Emm. I'd never heard her speak with such forcefulness before.

"I based my novel on, Charles," she continues. "He is my, Heathcliff and we will live here together, forever," she simpers. "What do you say, Charlie?"

"Emily, my dear Emily Bronte, I thought I'd lost you on those hills my darling. I searched for years but couldn't find you." Locking hands, they sit down at the table, staring into each other's eyes, oblivious to their surroundings.

"Oh, Emily," he whispers.

"Oh, Charles," she sighs.

"Oh god," I cry. "It's enough to make a ghost puke."

Turning back to Mary, I ask, "What if we share the bookshop somehow?"

"No way," replies Mary. "I am not sharing with you."

"You are so stubborn, Mary Shelly, I've a good mind to ..."

"Stop, that's enough of that, you're giving me a headache with your childish behaviour." The words boom from Daffy's mouth.

Astonished by the tone of her voice, we stop and stare.

"It's me, you fools, Du Maurier."

"Oh, my goodness," I gasp and like a fawning teenager stutter, "Daphne Du Maurier, I loved 'Rebecca.' Read it here one night just after publication. Couldn't put it down. Very, very good. Had me guessing all the way, nearly as exciting as the Pit and the Pendulum, but, not quiet there."

"Think you're so clever, don't you, Edgar? Well, let me tell you, my book has been made into a film. And, as physiological thrillers go, beats yours hands down. And if you don't behave, I'll call in the big guns."

"I am a big gun and my story was made into a film before yours. Look at all my books," I shout, pointing to the shelves. You only ever wrote one popular book."

"Not true. What about 'Jamaica Inn, The Birds, My Cousin ...?"

"Like I say, only one popular one."

"Vile man," she spits.

Trance-like, Art bellows, "I am the big gun. Knighted by King Edward VII, many years ago, you don't get much bigger than that."

We all turn to stare at Art.

"Who is it?" Mary asks.

"Who is it?" I mock, "only the greatest crime writer the world has ever known, Sir Arthur Conan Doyle. Don't you know anything, Mary?"

“Shut up, Pooy,” she says sticking her tongue out in a most unladylike fashion.

“Great to meet everyone,” Arthur says. “But, as I see it, we have a problem here.”

“No shit, Sherlock,” Du Maurier replies.

Ignoring her, he carries on, “Everyone wants to dwell in this bookshop so, why don’t we take turns? Mary, you could have Monday and Tuesday. Daphne you...

“Wait a minute,” I shout, holding my hand up. “This is my home, my bookshop, my place. Guys please, take a moment to consider my predicament. It’s where I glide, hover, spook and vaporise. You have no right to take it from me. I want you all to leave.”

“You’ve had well over a hundred years here. It’s time to move over and let others have a go,” says Sir Arthur.

“I don’t think so,” I start to say as the others, in frenzy, lift their hands and point towards me, chanting together, “OUT, OUT, OUT, OUT.”

Powerful forces grab at my cloak and shove me through the brick wall. I land on my bottom on the street outside. Bruised and embarrassed, I am about to leave, when the upstairs window opens and Mary cackles, “Mind your head, Pooy, bucketful coming your way.”

Behind me I hear the shop door open and turning around see Charlie, Emm, Daffy and Art, running for their lives, beyond them the ugly, contorted faces of people I once called friends, peer out of the windows.

Half-heartedly I try to warn them as Mary’s little present falls from above.

Too late, the contents of the bucket rain down on their heads. Maybe next time they’ll think twice about messing with the unknown.

Grinning, I drift off along the road in search of a new home.

For Rory with Love

By Jackie Skipp

Forever parted by that final door, I dream you live
Over Rainbow Bridge, the imaginary dog heaven that brings
Raw comfort for heartbroken owners left behind.

Rory, ragtag rascal of a dog
Overseas stray, your need found me.
Ready to give you the love and warmth you'd never known
Years went by while you gave me more than I could ever offer you.

Why are we never ready when that time has to come?
In bits as we spend those final moments, watching precious souls slip away,
Transcending earthly pains and the makeshift garden grave to travel into the unknown.
Hope you're safe, my little friend.

Loneliness fills the place where you lived for so long.
Overwhelming, unbearable, until eventually I see.
Voids are only physical; you'll never leave me.
Even in an empty house, my heart brims full of memories.

JUST BRICKS AND MORTAR

By Ann Evans

Moving house inspired this story by Ann.

She was trapped. Emma realised she was trapped in a loveless marriage after the first few weeks. And not just loveless, it was a violent and dangerous marriage. He was manipulative and unforgiving, metering out punishment for burnt dinners and creased shirts, then always remorseful.

As if attached to an invisible rope, he would drag her back when she tried to escape. Finally, that rope had been stretched too far and for too long. One day it snapped, and Emma was catapulted to freedom, far enough to escape completely, to leave no trail.

For months afterwards she feared he would find her. Trap her like a butterfly in a net and the misery would go on. She constantly looked back over her shoulder; waking in the night, afraid; relieved to find she was still free.

Like a butterfly Emma had flitted from place to place, from one bedsit to another, from one job to another, from one town to another, allowing the trail to go cold so he could never trace her.

Three years later and the divorce absolute, Emma finally felt safe enough to settle. Now she stood in the rain outside the house she was to rent for the next year. It looked a quirky old building with tall ornate chimney pots. But its windows were double-glazed, and the facade covered in pebble-dashing, like a warm, grey overcoat.

The front garden was windowsill-high with weeds, but that would be fun, she would buy shears and spend warm spring days bringing it to order.

The estate agent arrived, huddled under an umbrella. “Morning. Nasty day.”

“It’s a wonderful day,” Emma declared, loving the wind and rain in her face. She felt free. Nevertheless, she was glad to get indoors.

“It needs work,” the agent remarked.

“So I see,” she agreed, finding cupboards full of rubbish and peeling wallpaper that was decades old. There were broken hinges on cupboard doors, so they hung at crooked angles. One bedroom had a charred spot on the floorboards as if squatters had lit a fire when electricity and gas had been turned off.

But there was no smell of damp, no dark patches of mould. She touched a wall, it felt solid, safe. As she explored, she felt the strength and sturdiness of the building. Nothing creaked. There were no shadowy corners where someone could lurk. It just felt neglected and unloved.

“Why hasn’t the owner redecorated?” she asked, already planning colour schemes and décor. “Landlords have to keep properties up to scratch, don’t they?”

The agent consulted his notes. “It meets the regulations - new wiring, gas and boilers good as new. Owner’s probably disillusioned. It’s one of those properties where no one stays long. That’s why the rent is so cheap.”

“I can redecorate, can’t I? Some landlords won’t allow it.”

“Do what you want to it – well not structurally, but cosmetically.”

“I can’t wait!”

Emma moved in the following Monday. She hadn’t amassed many possessions since leaving the marital home. At the time, she had left with one suitcase and ran.

With her car unloaded, she closed the front door on the outside world and sighed. The house seemed to sigh too. They had both been neglected and badly treated over the years. Now they would recover together.

She cleaned and scrubbed, stripped away dull wallpaper and replaced it with pretty patterned paper, painted woodwork, fixed cheerful lampshades to bare bulbs and finally hung new curtains. They framed the sparkling windows like gorgeous eyelashes around joyful eyes.

She was never cold, the sturdy walls kept out the draughts and chill of winter. Returning home from work every evening, bringing another ornament or utensil to add to her home, the house welcomed her. She spoke to it all the time.

"Hello house! I'm home, have you missed me?"

One day she thought she heard it sigh, "Welcome home, Emma."

She laughed at her whimsical thoughts. Yet always she felt safe, cocooned in her happy home.

Each night as she turned off the lights, she said goodnight to the house. It was like a best friend. Sometimes she heard it say, "Goodnight, Emma."

Occasionally she wondered if the house was haunted, although there was no cold shivery presence. No, there were no ghosts. It was just the house itself speaking to her, nothing to be afraid of.

Out of interest she researched its history. It had been built in 1902 and the first family – the Fletchers, had lived here until after the Second World War. Then no mention of them and the house changed ownership time and again. Emma often wondered about the family who had cherished this house for over forty years.

Standing at the cooker, preparing dinner, she spoke out loud, "Are you still here? Are you watching over me? Are you pleased with how your home looks again?"

She listened, straining to hear any whisperings. There was no sound. No ghostly voices. She laughed and felt the house laughing with her. She spoke to the house instead. "No. No ghosts, just us."

She heard an echo. "Yes, just us."

As summer approached, Emma threw open the windows. Fresh summer fragrances filled the house. Her gardens were neat and tidy now. At first, she'd been daunted by the jungle of brambles. It had taken weeks of back-breaking work, yet it excited her to unearthing red brick pathways and traces of vegetable and rose gardens beneath the thorny weeds. And a child's lead soldier, remnants from when the Fletchers lived here, maybe. She'd washed the toy and placed it on her windowsill.

Standing in her garden she gazed up at the house. She imagined its façade as a kindly face looking down at her, like a mother gazing at its child, with love. No wonder the Fletchers had stayed so long. This was a safe dwelling.

Arranging flowers in a vase and placing them on the windowsill, she ran her hand down the window frame, as if stroking a loved one's cheek. "You haven't been treated so well these last few years, have you? Not since the Fletchers left. Do you miss them?"

From nowhere a trickle of rainwater ran down the windowpane.

Puzzled, Emma took a cloth and went outside. Perhaps a guttering was leaking although there had been no rain for weeks.

She wiped away the small stream of water, not knowing where it had seeped from. It was almost like wiping away a tear.

"Don't cry," she whispered. "I'm here now."

November was wet and windy, and Emma was eager to get indoors after work. For some reason the key refused to turn. Puzzled, she twisted and pushed but to no avail. hoping she could get in the back way, she hurried into her garden. She spotted the broken kitchen window instantly - broken and prised open.

Her blood ran cold. She backed away, fumbling for her phone, aware of noises coming from inside. Shakily she rang 999.

Police cars arrived within minutes. Officers swarmed around her house. Emma ventured near and informed them who she was.

"Have you got the key, love? Rather get in through the door than the window."

She handed it to him. "It won't open. I think they've put the latch down."

He opened the door easily however and eventually two teenage boys were led away in handcuffs.

Later Emma telephoned an emergency glazer, and while he fixed her damaged window, she cleaned up the mess. She was thankful they hadn't trashed the place. It was just drawers turned out, looking for money probably, nothing that couldn't be put right.

Later, in the middle of the night she awoke heart pounding, imagining intruders in her room. Just imagination, she realised thankfully. Then something dawned on her. The key had turned for the policeman, yet not for her.

"You didn't want me to walk in on them, did you?" she whispered to the house. "Thank you."

Turning over, she went back to sleep.

Her year's lease was nearly up. She sat reading the contract, pondering her choices. She didn't want to rent forever. The divorce settlement had provided a bit of money, and with such a low rent, she'd managed to save enough for a deposit on a house, something newer perhaps.

She browsed the property pages in the newspaper. There were quite a few houses within her range. It wouldn't hurt to take a look

Grabbing her coat, she noticed it was pouring with rain. "Oh, when did that start?"

She peered out. It was an absolute deluge. Oddly though, there was no sound of rain hammering against her windows. It wasn't going to stop her and pulling up her hood she tried to open the front door.

"Not again!" It was stuck fast again. She tugged and twisted – all in vein.

An uncomfortable sense of claustrophobia descended on her. Determined not to panic, she went to the back door. That refused to open too.

She tried again and again, finally kicking the door in frustration. Still it remained locked. Heart thumping, she tried to open a window. It refused to budge. She was sealed in – trapped.

Panicking now, she found her mobile. There was no signal.

"This is ridiculous!"

The windows continued to stream with water. She ran to the front again and peered out through the torrent. Passers-by distorted by the water glanced her way. But they weren't dashing along, head bent against the rain. No one even had an umbrella up.

Realisation hit her. It wasn't raining at all. She slumped down into a chair. Her head spinning, heart hammering.

The house was crying.

She sat for a long while, thinking. Rational thoughts to begin with. She would smash a window and escape. She wouldn't be trapped, not again, and definitely not by bricks and mortar. Only this house was more than that, and there was an ache in her heart as she felt its sorrow. "You don't want me to leave, do you?"

Understanding now, she walked slowly from room to room, her panic subsiding. She touched the walls, the door frames, ran her hands over the alcoves and chimney breasts. They seemed to touch her back, like a caress.

Gradually the streaming water ceased. She took a towel and walked to the door. It opened. She knew it would.

Stepping outside she stretched up and wiped away the water - dried away all the tears.

Returning indoors she didn't hesitate in closing the door behind her. She picked up her phone. She knew there would be a signal, and she rang her estate agent.

"It's about this house," Emma said after introducing herself. "My lease is almost up."

"Let me get your file."

Emma walked to the back door, touched the handle. She spoke softly. "You can't hold me against my will, you know."

Another trickle of water ran down the windowpane. But when she turned the handle, the door opened.

She stood in the open doorway as a voice came back on the line. "Hello, yes your lease is up at the end of the month. You'll be leaving then?"

Her eyes fluttered shut. The strangest silence settled over the house, as if it was holding its breath. She heard it breathe a sigh as she said, "Goodness me no! I'm ringing to ask...if I could buy this house!"

"Well! I wasn't expecting that. Are you sure? I'm pretty certain the owner would love to get it off his hands."

She relaxed against the door frame, feeling the sturdiness of the building. Feeling its protection. Her heart soared. "I'm sure."

The estate agent sounded delighted. "Well, that is good news. Now you're certain about this?"

"Absolutely," said Emma, returning indoors and clicking the door shut. "I love this house."

She didn't mention that the house loved her back.

RIBBONS

By Marilyn Pemberton

A 3-word class exercise prompted Marilyn to write this. The 3 random words were: Popular, Feathery, Ribbons.

She was the sort of girl who was always surrounded by fawning girls and boys, her smile was the broadest, revealing the whitest of perfect teeth; she had the loudest of voices that she used to share her opinions to which everyone always nodded in awed agreement. She was, I admit, the prettiest girl in the class and always won the "Miss Popular of the Year" competition. I hated her with every breath in my body and every fibre of my being.

I was short, my eyes came to her ample chest and I was twice as wide as her. Her hair was thick and long, mine was, at best, elfin and feathery, at worst short and greasy. I had my own opinions, but no-one ever listened to me. I was invisible to them; they didn't even know my name.

I despised her and her band of followers, but how I longed to be her. How I longed to be looked at by boys with puppy-dog eyes, who would willingly die for me. How I longed for everyone to hang onto my every simpering word and to swoon if I so much as smiled at them.

Each day she wore a different coloured ribbon at the end of her long plait. They found one wrapped round her beautiful swan-like neck.

She didn't look so pretty then.

THE ROSE VASE

By Ann Evans

The class exercise was to create a story around 3 randomly chosen words. They were: Kiln, Beaker, Ram.

It had become something of an obsession – the search. The need to keep looking. Walking towards the bustling car boot sale, Deidre turned to glance back at the rows of terraced houses and the tall chimneys of the potteries on the skyline. Years ago, those chimneys would have been smoking from the fires heating the kilns. The pottery business was all but dead now though.

Her grandparents and great grandparents had lived in those terraced houses. The Potteries were the main industry in this town. She'd seen the family photographs of skilled artisans sitting at their potter's wheels, turning out bone china plates and vases and figurines.

Deirdre heaved a sigh. It was sad to see the industry dying out, the potteries closing one after another. Everything was made in Hong Kong these days. Mass produced, churned out on conveyor belts. The art of the potter long gone.

The car boot sale was in full swing. She mingled. The buzz of excitement inside her growing. You never knew what you'd come across. A real bargain maybe, or a forgotten treasure. It was exciting.

She browsed, stopping every now and then if something caught her eye. She'd study the object for a hallmark or a maker's name. She watched the antique programmes on the television all the time – *Flog It, Antiques Roadshow, Cash in the Attic*, she watched them all. You could get a good education in antiques and collectables by watching the telly. Oh, and she liked the soaps, a bit of drama, a bit of make believe. They were good too.

Something caught her eye, stopping her in her tracks. A sky-blue vase, hand painted and decorated with pink roses. As she reached for it, another hand snatched it up.

"Oh! You beat me to it," Deidre said, unable to hide the sadness in her voice.

The man holding the vase turned it over in his hand, reading the maker's name underneath. He looked pleased with himself. "Made right here in the Potteries, Claymore 1914."

"Yes, I know," Deirdre answered, gazing at it with love.

"Very collectable," he said out the corner of his mouth, not wanting the stall holder to realise he was holding something of value.

"No doubt," said Deirdre turning wistful eyes at the man. "And has the artist signed it?"

He looked again.

"There," Deidre gestured, pointing at the tiny signature fired into the glaze of the ornament. "Albert Claymore. He was the nephew of John Claymore senior – my great grandfather."

The man and the stall holder both looked astounded at her. "Really?"

Deirdre nodded. "May I hold it?"

The man handed it to her, and she held it lovingly in her hands.

"My great grandmother told me the story behind the rose vase. He made these in her honour. Very few were made. Maybe only one."

"You don't say?"

"Yes. With the First World War just started, Great Granddad Albert as a young man had made up his mind to enlist and go off to fight for King and country. My great grandma was expecting their first child – their only child, as it turned out. After his final day at the pottery before he went off to war, he told her that he'd made a vase especially for her. It was sky-blue like her eyes and was patterned with pink roses – pink like her cheeks. And the rose..." Deirdre smiled at the man and the stall holder. "Rose, because that was her name."

"That's really nice," said the man. "I'm right glad you told me that. A bit of provenance. It's good to have the history behind a piece of pottery."

"Yes," Deirdre agreed, running her fingers over the glaze, her eyes misting a little. "This was made with love – his love for a woman, a wife, a mother – my great grandmother." She heaved a sigh. "Albert never saw their son. You see, he never came home from the war. Killed in action."

"Oh! Well that is a shame." The man lowered his head as a mark of respect. Two or three other people who had stopped to listen began murmuring about the follies of war.

"So how come this isn't a family heirloom?" the stall holder wanted to know.

"It should have been," agreed Deirdre. "But with Albert being killed, poor Rose was quite beside herself, so the story goes. With a child on the way, she had more important things to think about. She forgot all about the vase that her dear husband had made in her honour. It was years and years later when she thought about what he'd said. By then, the vase was long gone. Relatives doubted its existence even. It became something of an urban myth."

She breathed deeply as she handed it back to the man. "But it does exist! And here's the proof."

The man held it reverently. Then with a saintly look on his face he placed it back into Deidre's hands. "I can't buy this now. You need to have it. It's part of your family's history."

"But you saw it first!" Deirdre protested. "You'd have happily bought it if I hadn't spoken up. Please don't let me ruin things for you."

"Madam, this has just made my day. Nothing would give me more pleasure than to see this back where it belongs. In the Claymore family's possession, as it was intended."

Deidre blinked back the tears. "You're very kind, but I probably couldn't afford to buy it anyway."

The stall holder looked at the vase, then at the man, and then at Deidre. "Well, I was going to ask fifteen..." He saw the expression on the man's face. "Ten then... Oh, all right, a fiver."

"If you're sure," said Deirdre. "Would you hold it for me again, while I see if I've any money." She scrambled for her purse and found four pound fifty. "Oh! Not quite enough."

With a resigned look on his face the stall holder held out a beaker full of change. "Go on then. Chuck what you've got into my money pot."

She dropped the coins in. "I can't tell you how overjoyed I am. If only Great Grandma Rose was still around. I know, I'll put flowers in it and take it to her grave."

"Y'know, that's really touching," said the stall holder.

The man agreed. "Isn't that the great thing about these kind of sales? It isn't just about making a quid here or a quid there. It's stories like this that really touch the heart. Good on you, m'dear."

Smiling at them both, and clutching the vase to her chest, Deirdre walked back to the bus stop and home.

Two weeks later, she headed back into town. It was no wonder it had become a bit of an obsession. The excited buzz she felt inside was like a drug. She walked quickly down the High Street and straight in through the door of the building. She picked up the small printed brochure and ran her finger down the list of items.

There it was, Lot number 24, a rare Claymore Rose Vase dated 1914, painted by the artist Albert Claymore, nephew of John Claymore senior, factory owner.

The auction house was rammed with prospective buyers.

The bidding for the vase began at two hundred pounds. Deidre knew it would the second she clapped eyes on it.

She smiled to herself as the bidding war got under way. Those TV antique programmes came in useful. But then so did TV drama. She was getting quite good at making up stories these days.

The Lake

By Marilyn Pemberton

A photograph of a lake inspired Marilyn to write this short piece.

We started out as being six - three girls and three boys. We sat on the water's edge, enjoying the sun on our faces, the food in our bellies and each other's company. We weren't couples, not really, but we did seem to split into pairs, just temporarily for the afternoon, though for some it would be for eternity. We had never been here before but had come across the lake during a walk through the forest. Though it was a lovely summer's day, the water was black and didn't reflect the fluffy clouds that sauntered across the blue sky.

Tom was ever the restless one and as the rest of us dozed, he wandered off to explore, dragging Emily with him. I was actually dropping off to sleep when I was startled awake by a shout.

"I've found a boat! Who's for a row on the lake?"

I really couldn't be bothered, nor could my partner Bob, who was in a deep sleep, but the other two roused themselves and very soon I heard the sound of rows creaking, girls giggling and boys puffing. I sat on a rock and watched, wondering idly why I couldn't also hear the sound of the splashing as they inexpertly tried to row. The water seemed thick, like treacle and I was intrigued at how quickly the boat seemed to travel, despite the little actual effort being made.

I had to pinch myself to check I was awake, but I was right - the water was forming shapes of its own accord. Forms like black hands were reaching up and grabbing for the oars, creeping up the side of the boat. I screamed at them, but they didn't seem to hear me. They were laughing at something Tom had said, until one of the hands reached the edge of the boat and took hold of Emily's arm. Her laugh turned into a scream as she was pulled over the edge and slowly, ever so slowly, pulled into the blackness.

The others didn't do anything; it was if they were frozen. Then suddenly there was panic, and the boys tried to row away, but the hands grabbed the oars off them and they were soon left floundering about. The water around the boat seemed to heave and now shapes, human and yet not human, rose and hung onto just one side of the boat, tipping it down until by force of gravity, the three slid screaming into open arms that embraced them lovingly before pulling them into the deep.

I stood watching, horrified, as the waters settled back down, and I wondered if I had dreamt everything. I turned to Bob, who was still snoring. Had the others even been there? Was I going mad? Was I already mad?

LOVER'S LAKE

By Mary Ogilvie

The class exercise was to feature a lake.

The lovers gazed into each other's eyes, finally reunited, together at last.

Although they were born into families of opposite clans, they were thrown together in youth. But Matilda, the only child of the High Chieftain was betrothed to an older man of great wealth.

"No, Father. I will not marry him. I have no love for him. Please let it not be."

She had begged and pleaded with her father, but to no avail.

Her father was adamant. The wedding would go ahead.

The night before the wedding, Matilda had walked down to the lake, her place of comfort. There, she waited for her lover, to bid farewell to him. To kiss one last time.

There was no sign of him.

Beside herself with despair and misery, she walked slowly into the lake.

Heartbroken, her lover blamed himself for her death. Had he not been late...
Unable to contain his grief, he submitted himself to the same fate.

On clear nights, some say the silhouettes of two lovers can be seen together, standing together, locked in a loving embrace, beside the lake.

CRACKPOT

By Bec Woods

The class exercise was to write a story using these 3 random words: Kiln, Beaker, Ram.

She bet Demi Moore didn't have this problem when she was throwing pots. Chrissie Muldoon tried to make the lump of clay in front of her look like something recognisable and not just to her.

When her husband Jack had brought a cup of tea to her studio he'd tried to be encouraging "I like your corkscrew thing."

"It's a ram," Chrissie had corrected him and then, when he'd looked even more puzzled, "You know, symbol for Aries." That had completely lost him, and he made a quick exit before any more clay was thrown.

So, Chrissie had started again, closing her eyes like the woman in Lionel Richie's video and hoping that she would produce an equally stunning piece of art. But when she opened her eyes the form in front of her looked more like a sci-fi monster.

Sitting back on her stool she reached for the beaker that Jack had brought in. That had been another of her creations, though originally with a handle. Unfortunately, the handle hadn't taken properly and had come away from the mug the first time she'd used it – hot tea everywhere and pride bruised.

Perhaps she wasn't cut out for pottery, like she hadn't been cut out for sewing or baking. "Damn you!" she said to the television that sat at the end of the workbench. "Making me think I can do all these things easily."

Looking around she saw the pile of cookery books

in the corner, topped by a selection of cake tins and a bolt of colourful fabric that was going to be a couture dress.

In irritation she punched the 'on' button and was immediately faced with Alan Sugar, a stern-faced Sid James with his entrepreneur carry on. Mind you she thought, perhaps he's got something...

And turning to the kiln in the corner she put down her tea and pointing a finger said, "You're fired!"

ONE SUMMER'S EVENING

By Marilyn Pemberton

Some members of the class entered a competition with the theme of 'The door closing'.

It was a still summer's evening; there was no breath of air to move the heat that wrapped itself round me. When I came to the wood its coolness tempted me and I was drawn ever inwards in search of its cold core. I found, instead, an empty wooden lodge. There were tiles missing off the roof, the windows were boarded up and weeds grew from every conceivable crevice. Someone had lived there once; there was a hammock on the veranda, the cushions rotten and mouldy. There were the remains of a vegetable patch that now grew nothing but dandelions and daisies.

I mounted the steps, avoiding the rotten planks. The door was warped and couldn't close properly but after a hard push I was able to open it. Inside, it was gloriously cool. There were piles of leaves in all the corners and a thick layer of dust lay over the few bits of broken furniture that had been left behind. It smelt of damp earth and dust and animal droppings.

There was no electricity, of course, but I had a flashlight and by its beam I wondered around, feeling sad at what happiness may have once been felt there. I didn't expect the cellar to reveal any treasures, but I decided to take a peek. I opened the door wide, propping it open with a large stone. The light revealed nothing but an empty room and I was just about to turn back when I heard footsteps, a tinkle of laughter and the bang as the door was decisively shut.

PLENTY OF FISH

By Maxine Burns

Maxine wrote on the same theme of 'a door closing'.

Rory looked across the park from his fifth-floor balcony for the third time in half an hour. He'd seen a couple of joggers, a teenager walking a dog, her head down, earphones in, tinny music drifting from her phone. An old granny hurrying home with her shopping. There was no sign of the man he was expecting.

He stalked back into the living room, picked up his phone and tapped out the now familiar number.

"It's me again," he roared. "Where's the bloody electrician? You said he'd be here in a couple of minutes and that was half an hour ago."

The calm voice on the line was drowned out by the doorbell buzzing in the hall.

"Forget it, he's here." Rory said, cutting the call, striding across the sitting room, into the hall, flinging open the front door.

"Where the bloody..." he stopped mid-sentence and gaped at the woman standing on his doorstep with a large leather bag in her hand and a big smile on her face.

"Who the pigging hell are you?" he snarled, moving his head to look beyond her, "and where's the bloody electrician?"

There was a short silent as she looked him up and down. She raised an eyebrow and said, "I think you'll find that's me," then pushed past him into the hall.

"Hang on a minute," said Rory, grabbing hold of her.

She stopped abruptly and looked pointedly at his hand on her arm.

Rory blushed and let go. "Sorry," he stammered, "but I was expecting..."

"A man?" she said, "sorry to disappoint."

Rory stepped away and straightened his back in an attempt to regain his equilibrium. "I'm not sure I'm comfortable with this," he said, folding his arms for good measure.

"With what? Me?"

Rory nodded. "Are you qualified," he asked, "can you fix it?"

"Yes and yes," she said. "Now, do you want to show me where the boiler is?"

Rory paused, then with a sigh pointed to the ceiling. "It's in the attic."

"Great," she said, marching past him, "You can make me a cup of tea. I always work better with a drink."

Cheeky cow, thought Rory as he filled the kettle and switched it on, watching closely as she pulled the ladder down, grabbed her tool bag and climbed up into the attic. Nice backside, though.

"You can go and sit down, if you like," she called, "Relax. I won't blow anything up. Promise."

"No thanks, I'll wait here." Rory answered. He wasn't taking any chances.

Sally sneaked a look through the attic entrance. Rory was busy making the tea. She pulled her head back sharply as he glanced up. What a horrible man, she thought. What on earth had Suzanne seen in him? She opened her bag and pulled out the large, plastic container of raw fish she had brought with her.

Tiptoeing silently around the junk filled space, she placed some of the cold, slimy cod heads behind an old sideboard, more between the wooden beams, then tucked the remainder at the bottom of a large box containing

Christmas decorations. Opening a bag of frozen prawns, she dropped them, a few at a time, through tiny holes in the wooden flooring.

Sally sat back on her heels and smiled, pleased with her work. Finally, she raised the heating, then snapped the thermostat. All done. She'd give a lot to smell this place in a week or two. That would teach him to mess with Suzanne, her sister. Leading her on, breaking her heart. Moving on without giving her a second thought.

Sally made her way carefully back down the ladder. Rory was in the kitchen, cooking his dinner. Popping her head around the door, she said, "All done. Phone in if you have any other problems." She glanced at the contents of the pan. He was frying a fillet of cod.

"Enjoy your dinner," she called out with a grin, as she closed the door behind her.

THE DOOR

By Catherine Wilson

A memory from the past concerning a mysterious door inspired this story from Catherine.

The alarm rang loudly. I pressed the snooze button to give me another hour, but sleep wouldn't come. Slumping out of bed, I yawned myself across the room and leaned on the windowsill. Bright moonlight rendered the scruffy gardens and outbuildings pearly clean.

Leaning further out, my sleepy eyes drifted to the kitchen, coalhouse and outside toilet, on the cobbled yard below. Shivering in the icy morning, my warm bed invited me back. I turned and stopped. My subconscious early morning brain had registered something amiss. Wiping my eyes on the edge of the curtain I blinked them clear. Nothing odd there, but my gut said...*Look!*

I looked, counting carefully: kitchen door, one; coalhouse door, two; toilet door, three – and another... I stared.

Yes, another door I hadn't noticed before, and I'd lived here for nearly three years.

Now wide awake I grabbed a dressing gown and crept down the creaky winding stairs avoiding the vacuum cleaner stored at the bottom. Reaching the back door, I slipped my feet into a pair of boots and unlocked it quietly, trying not to waken my friend who rented the house with me. The clumsy boots sent a row of milk bottles smashing across the cobbles. I froze, but even next door's yappy dog didn't bark.

The doors glinted dully in the moonlight and the new one unlatched easily into a tiny vestibule. I gingerly pushed the glass door in front of me with a finger. It swished open into a large carpeted, furnished room with a kitchen at one end.

Incredulous, mouth wide open, I wondered if my Scrooge of a landlady knew about this.

Of course, she does, I thought, and our house so sparsely furnished considering the rent we pay.

Wandering around I tucked a couple of fat cushions under my arms planning to come back with my friend and substitute a pair of these comfy chairs for our dog-eared ones.

Back in the kitchen, I kicked off the boots. I was sparking with excitement. I threw the cushions onto the sofa in the lounge and made my way back to bed knowing I'd never get to sleep again.

The alarm rang loudly. I switched it off, surprised that I had slept. I dressed quickly, needing to see my housemate, before work.

"Come and see what I've found," I said excitedly, opening the door and stepping out, carefully avoiding the milk bottles lined up on the step. I pointed.

"What do you think of tha..." I stopped, staring at three peeling doors. I tried to speak.

"For goodness sake stop messing about and shut that door, it's freezing." Crossly my housemate pulled me indoors. "And what are my new boots doing out here?"

I told her what I'd seen.

"Only a dream." She passed me some coffee. "All that cheese last night – Oh, and two bottles of wine."

Laughing as I protested, she went through to the lounge.

"Come on, we'll miss the, er... Hey, where did these cushions come from?"

UNLOCKED

By Ella Cook

A closed door inspired this story from Ella.

Niamh stared at the note in horror. She'd been behind the locked door for so long that she thought everyone had forgotten her. It was what she would have preferred. She didn't want anything to do with the outside world and was happy that she seemed to have vanished from their thoughts.

Food and rubbish all passed through the little hatch in the wall, via the decontamination chamber she'd had specially installed.

When she'd first started to pull away from the world, people had worried and fussed. Family, friends, and eventually the healthcare team had come to visit – trying to pry her out of her self-imposed prison. But Niamh had never viewed the walls of her apartment in those terms. Rather than imprisoning her, they let her feel free.

Free from the worry of dealing with the outside world and all its horrors and germs. She wasn't lonely. Her virtual interactions suited her just fine.

And yet now, somehow, someone had pushed a note through her door. It was just a piece of lavender paper, folded in two. Clearly it hadn't been through the mail system. Which meant someone had somehow made it through the front door, gained access to the private stairway, and walked all the way to the top floor to slip it under her door.

There was nothing for it. She couldn't leave it sitting there, spreading who knew what germs throughout her home. Taking a deep breath, she retrieved a set of disposable gloves from underneath the sink and snapped them on with practiced ease. She held her breath, and gingerly picked up the scrap of paper.

Brightly coloured crayoned balloons and cakes festooned the paper – an invitation to a child's party. And inside, alongside the usual details, a single word picked out in rainbow hopefulness.

Please.

As she traced her fingers over crayon, she could have sworn she heard laughter in the hall, and the slow, creaking as the door closed.

Something inside her twisted, and a smile played around her lips as she slowly reached for the key.

ATTACK!

By Ann Evans

Ann also wrote on the theme of 'a door closing'.

Kathy remembered little about the attack that left her fighting for her life. The shadowy figure had come from nowhere as she walked home from work. Then came a terrific pain and blood pouring down her face.

She remembered tasting mud, and a smell – a pleasant cologne which seemed at odds being worn by such a heinous beast. She remembered his voice too as his overbearing presence engulfed her, violated her. "There's a good girl," he breathed over and over, as she fought against the dreadful sensation of blacking out – of dying.

She *had* blacked out, mercifully really. But although left for dead along that muddy track, she had survived. Weeks on life support, months gradually recovering before returning to work. Ironically, she was a nurse at the hospital. Their care and support had pulled her through.

Back at work now, everybody wanted to know if the police had caught her attacker yet.

"Not yet," she told them, doubting they ever would.

After all she'd gone through, she almost laughed at her own clumsiness when she twisted her ankle while on duty. The porter fetched her a wheelchair to take her down to
A & E.

He was middle aged and smelt nice she noticed as he helped her into the wheelchair.

"There's a good girl," he said softly as the ward doors closed behind her and he pushed her towards the long, lonely corridor.

FAMILY SECRETS

By Margaret Mather

A closed door proved inspirational for Margaret too.

Childhood recollections threaten to overwhelm me as I fumble with the front door latch. Stepping inside my parents' house for the last time, hits me like a sudden burst of hailstones on a clear spring day and I hesitate, unable to face reality.

Arranging my much-loved mother's funeral had kept me busy. And afterwards, clearing out the family home had taken up all of my energy. Only when finished had I succumbed to pent-up emotions and cried for days.

Now I stand in the cold, empty lounge, waiting for the estate agent to call, confirming the bank transfer.

Brushing my hand along the smooth, pine mantelpiece, I feel it shift. The movement reminds me of the many letters and cards that had fallen down the back. And how we'd rescued them, with the help of an old knitting needle.

Memories lift my sombre mood.

Poking out from behind the fireplace, a small, white envelope catches my eye, bending down, I retrieve it.

An old greetings card adorned with a smiling, fair-haired baby, wrapped securely in a pale blue blanket, rests snugly inside. Emblazoned across the front, 'Congratulations on the birth of your beautiful baby boy,' signed, Aunt Isobel.

Questions I will never know the answers to, swirl around my head. What happened to him? What was his name? Tears fall as I grieve for my unknown sibling.

My mobile rings, the caller verifies completion, time to go.

Clutching the precious card, I close the door and walk down the path for the last time.

1967: THE SUMMER OF LOVE

By Maxine Burns

The class were asked to write a non-fiction article.

In the spring of 1967, a movement born in San Francisco had soared across the Atlantic to land with a bang in London, bringing with it a revolution of ideas, music, fashion and descent. By the year's end the face of Britain had shifted dramatically, never to be the same again. Dividing the country just as Brexit is doing today.

Post war children had grown up with parents recovering from a war that had all but shattered the world. They'd suffered bitter winters in cold, bleak houses and food shortages. They vowed their children would never suffer the same deprivations and have better, more affluent lives.

By the time the sixties arrived, social conditions had improved. Slums were demolished and replaced with new, smarter housing, often high rises. Work was plentiful, therefore cash to purchase the smarter clothes, which filled the new shops in rebuilt and modernized city centres, was available.

Old and young were enjoying an improved lifestyle. They watched TV together. Family favourites such as *Coronation Street,* modern comedies like *Till death Do Us Part* and the new, scary *Doctor Who*. England had soundly beaten West Germany to claim the 1966 World cup. Many young people were taking the opportunity to attend university and prosperity beckoned the working classes like never before. Life was pretty good.

However, events at home and abroad were taking place that would have a profound effect on this young, better educated generation. In 1962 the Russian leader, Nikita Khrushchev and John F. Kennedy clashed over Khrushchev's decision to build nuclear missiles in Cuba, a short 50 miles from the coast of Florida. Kennedy responded by blockading Cuba with a circle of warships.

The resulting Cuban missile crisis caused the entire world to hold its breath and contemplate the spectre of imminent annihilation. After thirteen long days a deal was agreed and both sides stood down. Kennedy appeared on television and said, 'We all inhabit this small planet, we all breathe the same air and we are all mortal.'

The War in Vietnam started in 1955 and had escalated considerably by the mid '60's.
It was the first war to be covered by television. Each evening families watched as images of the horrific events taking place in Vietnam and Cambodia played on the screen. Crops decimated by the deadly chemical 'Agent Orange.' Women and children running, on fire due to being blasted with napalm – a modern weapon made from petrol and gel, enabling it to stick to the skin, causing severe burns. Young Americans – average age of 19 years, drafted straight from high school, returning home in body bags.

By 1967, many Americans had enough of their involvement in this dishonourable war and began to demand its end. School children who'd scanned the skies for nuclear rain and watched as a distant country was decimated, were ripe for change. They had got the message. They were mortal.

The restraints observed by previous generations, loosened. The idea of 'The Summer of Love' – the phrase that appeared for the first time in the *San Francisco Chronicle,* captured the imagination and heralded a voice audible only to the young. They could be heard at last and needed the world to listen. They gathered together at the heart of where it was all happening – London.

Politics became *cool*. The protest marches which took place in London, Paris and New York attracted thousands. The iconic peace symbol, 'Ban the Bomb' and the two-fingered peace sign was revitalised. A counterculture emerged. The Age of Aquarius had arrived.

Underpinning this movement was a wave of new, exciting bands, playing fresh, innovative music. Bands like Cream, Pink Floyd, Fleetwood Mac, and from the US, the Doors, Jefferson Airplane and Jimi Hendrix.

The Beatles enthusiastically embraced all things psychedelic, grew their hair, experimented with drugs and released *Sergeant Peppers Lonely Heart Club Band*, to rave reviews. John Lennon drove a psychedelic Rolls Royce. The sublime *A whiter shade of pale* shot to number one and Scott McKenzie's *San Francisco – Be sure to wear flowers in your hair* became the anthem of a generation.

One of the illegal offshore radio stations, Radio Caroline broadcast music continually, had millions of listeners and kick-started the careers of a new wave of young DJ's, including Kenney Everett and Tony Blackburn. The stuffy BBC were forced to capitulate and launched Radio 1.

Illegal drugs became fashionable, with cannabis the focus of many campaigns to legalize it. The Beatles were amongst various celebrities of the day, who signed a petition to this effect. Rolling Stones, Mick Jagger and Keith Richards were famously arrested and put on trial for the possession of illegal drugs.

The contraceptive pill allowed women to free themselves from erstwhile Victorian respectability and unwanted pregnancies. The abortion law was changed, and women no longer had to resort to unlawful, dangerous back street abortionists. The nuclear family began to evolve and embrace alternative values. Unmarried mothers were less likely to be stigmatised, marriage declined, and communal living flourished.

Popular films of the day were, *Bonnie and Clyde* and *The Graduate,* with much of the soundtrack written by Paul Simon and Art Garfunkel. The musical, *Hair,* premiered and received sensational reviews, fuelled by the nude scenes it contained.

Alternative newspapers and magazines were published, specifically aimed at the counterculture generation. The *International Times* covered the underground music scene and was radically political, featuring works by William Burroughs, Allen Ginsberg and Norman Mailer. *Rolling Stone Magazine*, founded in San Francisco, featured John Lennon on the cover of its first edition. 'Turn on, tune in, drop out' was the buzz phrase that defined the attitude of the counterculture movement.

Diverse religious practises were explored. Buddhism, transcendental meditation and Krishna consciousness amongst the favourites. The thoroughfares of London teemed with street vendors, selling the alternative magazines, beads, bangles, scarves, incense - all things Hippy. *Cranks,* London's first vegetarian restaurant, paved the way for a different way of eating. Meat was 'out,' lentils and nut cutlets were 'in.'

The Culture of the 60's heralded concepts and changes in society which resonate today. Heightened political awareness, Yoga and meditation, green values, attitudes towards social relationships, gay rights, are just a few which eventually became mainstream.

The confidence, daring and originality of the 1960's could help us all create a better world today.

All you need is love.

IN DEEP AND TROUBLED WATERS

By Jackie Skipp

A photograph of a canal towpath inspired Jackie to write this story.

"You need to think this through, Jodie." Leon's voice nagged at the back of Jodie's head as she trudged along the muddy canal path. She kept her eyes fixed ahead, trying to ignore him, but his words hit home. Had she thought it through? Had she been so incensed at being edged out of her life at home that rational thought had evaded her?

Today, she felt as though she had finally been totally erased. And if her stepfather had held the rubber in recent years, her mother certainly hadn't stopped him using it. No, she concluded, there was no further thinking to be done. Her stepfather would get his wish; he had pushed Jodie so far that she would take herself out of their lives completely.

"What are you going to do?" Leon's voice droned in her ears, submersing her thoughts.

Jodie slowed her step along the towpath as a young woman emerged from the pub ahead, carrying a large wicker basket. For a second, Jodie didn't recognise the sounds coming from inside the basket, then the heads appeared over the top. Two identical faces, only different in size and age; pink noses set in black and whites faces as startled green eyes peered towards her.

The smaller one mewed furiously, its kitten face stretched to reveal tiny needle-sharp teeth. The wicker basket drowned them – Jodie flinched at her own thoughts – but they were determined to be seen and heard. Jodie stared at the two black and white animals, as a distant sweet memory forged in her mind.

"How about this one?" her mother had asked brightly, kneeling down beside her as Jodie had looked past her mother's pointing finger and the confident kitten who greeted them boldly with a loud meow, to the smallest one cowering nervously behind her siblings.

"What are you going to call her?" her dad had asked, as they left the rescue centre, the nervous kitten safely ensconced in a brand new carrier.

Jodie had glanced at her mother timidly, sensing a lack of approval for her choice, before cocking her head to one side to study her new pet.

"Smudge!" she announced triumphantly, smiling at her father. "Because she's white with black smudges all over her."

Life had been that simple when she was six years old.

The woman frowned as Jodie stared wordlessly at the basket, then smiled uncertainly and made an attempt at conversation. "These two are ready for their tea."

Jodie looked into the face of the older cat and saw Smudge again. The little cat had soon found her feet and become playmate and confidante to Jodie through good times and bad. She had distracted her from the raised voices of her parents' arguments and slept curled around her head every night after Jodie's father left, seemingly oblivious to the wet tear-stained pillow under her fur.

By the time Smudge got sick, Jodie's dad was living on the barge he had bought after her parents' divorce and working away from home sporadically. The cat's fate was dependent on how much her mother was swayed by her boyfriend Ray, who had recently moved in, and hated cats. Jodie's attachment to her pet won her mother over initially and Smudge was taken to the vet to have an abscess removed from her side, but when another lump formed, Ray's arguments against what he called *throwing good money after bad,* were too strong and Smudge's next trip to the vet was to be put to sleep.

"It would have been cheaper to drown her." Ray's words as her mother brought home the little lifeless body wrapped in a towel had filled Jodie with hatred and anger which curdled with her adolescent pain and despair at the loss of her best friend.

Jodie felt her nails dig into her palms and her teeth pierce her lip as the bitter memory chewed into her again.

"I think she's expecting you to say something, Jodie." Leon hissed in her ear.

She rounded on him then. "Shut up, Leon."

The smile faded from the young woman's face and she turned and walked quickly away from the canal, around the corner of the pub.

Jodie took a few steps forward and watched as the woman crossed the pub car park and deposited the basket carefully in the boot of a jeep. The younger cat attempted to climb out of the basket while the elder one batted it back gently with a paw, an act of mild chastisement. As the woman drove away, Jodie watched, engulfed suddenly in a deadening mix of sadness, guilt and shame.

"You're scaring me. I don't even know what you're thinking any more. There was an undertone of panic in Leon's voice now. "*You* don't seem to know what you're thinking anymore!"

"I don't." Jodie's voice was flat as she forced her feet onwards along the wet path, splattering mud on the skirt of her uniform. It didn't matter. She wouldn't be wearing it again. Even if she stayed, she'd have to leave her after-school job at the vets. Her stepfather's letter from the DWP that day had put an end to that. Ray had lost his benefits and decided she had to give up school and get a 'proper job' to help support the family.

Ironically, she came to the bend of the river where Ray's life had changed so dramatically a few years ago. She remembered the police visits to her home, the story in the newspaper. He had been fishing on the towpath when he'd been attacked with a large rock.

There was no shortage of suspects; Ray was a quarrelsome man who had made many enemies throughout his life. Only days before the attack, he'd started a fight in the pub she'd just passed, which had ruined the birthday party of an elderly lady. He had been barred on the spot, but the lady's family were not satisfied, and several angry threats were subsequently made.

The police investigation dwelled heavily on the incident at the pub, but their enquiries fell flat, met with a wall of silence. No-one had seen anything or knew anything. The case was shelved, and so was Ray's life. The blow had caused brain damage that left him with slurred speech, loss of memory and regular seizures.

His condition had improved a little over the intervening years; Jodie suspected more so than he admitted. Ray had got used to sitting at home, drinking and betting on the horse racing he watched on TV while her mother worked 50 hours a week. If he had been unpleasant to Jodie before the attack, he had become unbearable since. She couldn't live with him anymore.

"I can't help you anymore. You know that." Leon's voice persisted. Jodie dropped her chin and began to hum, purposely shutting him out.

Her downcast eyes lifted when she came close to the little barge that had been her father's home for the last seven years. It's peeling green paint had been replaced by a serviceable navy blue and clean gingham curtains adorned the windows. The hatch was slightly open, and she took a deep breath as she climbed aboard.

"Dad?" She peered down into the narrow galley kitchen.

"Someone else needs to keep your secret now." Leo pleaded.

She crossed the kitchen into the living area and reached down to pick up the gilt- edged picture frame from beside the TV. Three faces smiled back at her – her own, her father's and Leon. A happy day spent on the boat like so many others.

She remembered her childish animosity towards her father and his son in the months before she was allowed to meet Leon. Her mother had poisoned her mind; embittered by the sudden discovery of her husband's long-standing affair and the child it had brought into the world two years before Jodie. She would have liked the end of her marriage to have seen the severing of all ties, but Jodie's father had fought for access and introduced the two children. A deep bond had formed between them, and Jodie forgot the word 'step' as she looked forward to weekends and spending time with her brother and father.

"Jodie, you know who you have to talk to." Leon's placid brown eyes surveyed her as his slim teenage frame leant against the door frame. She looked into a face no older than the face in the photo and saw a bleakness she had never associated with her brother.

She squeezed her eyes shut against the feeling of terrible loss and pain in the tiny room. Her body trembled and she swallowed twice before answering Leon. "I can't tell dad."

"Jodie? What's wrong, love? What can't you tell me?"

Jodie's vision was blurred with tears as her father came towards her, arms ready to envelop her. She felt the roughness of his heavy sweater against her cheek as he pressed her against him.

His voice dropped. “Who were you talking to?”

She heaved a sob, unable to tell him.

He pulled her closer to him.

And then the words were out in a rush. “Dad, I hit Ray, it was me!” She bit her lip. “I was going to push him into the river after I’d knocked him out, but I lost my nerve. I wanted him to drown, just like he said we should have done to Smudge when she was ill.”

She waited for her father’s reaction, expecting him to release her, push her away in shock. He didn’t.

She was unable to see the tears in her father’s eyes through her own, but she heard them in his voice. “It did cross my mind once, love. You were so unwell afterwards, and I knew how upset you’d been about Smudge....” He wiped his face with the back of his hand. “I should have talked to you, but then, well, with what happened to Leon.”

His body shuddered and she knew he was remembering the awful day he had let her steer the boat with him while his son had lain asleep at the back of the boat. Leon was a livewire who needed a watchful eye always, but she guessed that day her father had assumed that he couldn’t get up to much while he was fast asleep.

They never knew what happened. Leon just disappeared from the boat, and the following day, his body was dredged from the canal. It was as simple as that. As awful as that. As final as that.

Her father composed himself and eased himself away from her to look down into her face. “Have you told anyone else?”

"She steeled herself as her next words caught in her throat and she had to force them out. "Leon. I confided in Leon and he kept my secret until the day we lost him."

There was a silence that Jodie couldn't bear, and she broke it with the news she'd come to deliver.

"Dad, I'm leaving. I can't bear it there anymore."

Her words broke through the shock and his response was immediate. "Don't go. Come and live with me."

For a second she hesitated. "Are you sure? I'm messy."

"And who do you think you get that from?" He was grinning now, the happy face she associated with her childhood.

She dumped her bag on the bench-seat, noticing for the first time the white paper package her father had dropped there when he came in. The smell of salt and vinegar hit her nostrils, and she realised she was starving. "Are there enough chips for me?"

He nodded and reached to unwrap the package, nudging her to sit down on the seat as he dropped down next to her and placed the chips between them.

She smiled, feeling a lightness she hadn't experienced in many years. She looked towards the doorway. Leon was smiling too, a sad, sweet smile.

"Told you he'd understand." His voice was faint.

She looked back towards her dad and her new home and the sadness that had been around her for so long drifted away.

FAIRY TALES

By Margaret Mather

A class exercise in writing description inspired Margaret to write this delightful fairy tale.

"Granddad, there are no such things as fairies."

"Really? I think you'll find that there are, Tizzy," Granddad said rubbing his hand over the stubble on his chin.

"But, Granddad, if there are fairies, why can't I see them?"

"You can't see them, because they hide from children."

Granddad moved closer to Tizzy and bending down whispered in her ear, "They crawl inside upturned plant pots or scamper underneath the leaves of a bluebell when they hear children coming. Sometimes they disguise themselves as flowers."

Tizzy, fiddling with the wings of her fairy costume said, "Well, if they look like flowers, how can you tell what is and isn't a fairy, Granddad?"

"You can't. You need to see them for yourself. On the night of a full moon, when the clock strikes midnight, they play by the oak tree at the bottom of the garden. On such a night, with the moon as bright as a glitter ball, you can see fairies fluttering.

"They love to party. Nuts and blackberries with a drizzle of honey, are their favourite foods. They drink rainwater flavoured with raspberries from the garden. Each fairy wears a tiny dress made from lilac, lemon or pink coloured petals. Fireflies light up their wings and make them sparkle. Then they dance until the moon drops from the sky and the sun starts to rise."

Tizzy placed a thoughtful finger upon her lips then said, "What if it rains, Granddad?"

"Mmm, that's a tough one. I think they make umbrellas out of buttercups. Why don't you stay awake one night and see for yourself?"

Granddad smiled at Tizzy, safe in the knowledge that she could never stay awake that long.

Tizzy returned his smile and made a mental note to set her alarm tonight.

MAN AND DOG V WIND

By Marilyn Pemberton

A class exercise to create atmosphere on a cliff top inspired this piece of flash fiction.

John tightened his coat belt and pulled up his collar as meagre protection against the biting wind that blew horizontally off the sea, but he couldn't shelter from the sharp needles of sleet that stabbed at his cheeks. Toby was pulling at the lead, desperate to run off and explore the cliff-top smells.

Against his better judgement John let him go, praying that the malevolent wind wouldn't sweep up the little dog and hurl him into the maws of the hungry sea below. The wind, however, seemed intent on sacrificing John to the sea gods and he felt the invisible sinews wrap themselves around him and tug him towards the abyss.

His feet slipped in the mud and he was suddenly only inches away from the edge. The wind dropped, gathering its strength for the final assault and John took the opportunity to retreat to the relative safety of the rock face that bordered the inland side of the path.

He crouched down, holding tightly onto a protruding crag and waited for the wind to lose interest.

Toby! He had forgotten all about the little dog. He shouted out his name, but the wind took the words and threw them mockingly back at him. He shouted until he was hoarse but there was neither sight nor sound from the familiar shaggy mutt.

John's eyes watered from the ferocity of the wind, from anger at his own stupidity in coming onto the cliff in the first place, and from grief at the loss of his one remaining friend.

He closed his eyes and imagined himself back home, sitting by a roaring log fire, Beethoven playing quietly in the background, a glass of wine in one hand, the other caressing Toby's ears. He imagined himself dozing off and Toby nudging him, as he was wont to do when he considered that he was not getting the attention that he was due.

John smiled sadly to himself at the memory of Toby's constant head butting until his master gave in and started fondling him again. He could almost feel the coarse hair under his fingertips and hear the small bell which tinkled as Toby swooned in ecstasy.

Some time later, when the weather had eased, another dog walker came along the path and was horrified to find an old man crouching at the foot of the escarpment, as cold and wet as the rock itself, with a small, white dog by his side, whining and nudging the lifeless hand.

EVENINGS ON ABERSOCH BEACH

By Catherine Wilson

I loved to stroll on the lonely sands
When the trippers had drifted away,
And the mist rose up from a tide smoothed beach,
For the treasured last hours of a day.
When the sun dropped off the horizon;
And the world was a comforting grey

Then my toes would squelch in the cold wet sand
And my face felt the beat of the rain,
And the sea horses calmed to a gentler trot,
As the wild waves loosened their rein.
I could hear the song of the mermaids
And their loved ones' sweet refrain.

A SIREN'S CALL

By Mark Howland

Still on the theme of the sea, Mark has written this captivating tale.

"This time, I will reach her… " he recalled murmuring upon awakening earlier that morning, after another restless night's sleep.

Trudging through the wet shingle, Tom was certain he'd made the right decision, the only decision. Yet the unsettled emptiness wrestling within only seemed to intensify and its essence was to remain frustratingly, forever out of reach.

His foster parents hadn't approved of course, they couldn't understand why he had chosen to give up a perfectly good job in the city, only to leave it all behind and start over again somewhere new. But that hadn't dissuaded him. They had never understood him, how could they? Only this wasn't somewhere else, this was precisely where he needed to be. Tom couldn't explain it to anyone any better than he could explain it to himself. All he knew is that he was wholly consumed with an overwhelming desire to live by the sea.

All of his life he had been troubled by reoccurring dreams of the ocean and of haunting melodies that would find him weeping while he slept. As a child he had often tried to reach out to anyone, to find some way of fixing something he sensed broken inside, but who ever really listens to children? Tom realised from an early age, grownups only heard what they wanted to hear and at the first sign of anything problematic, they always concocted some poor excuse and promptly vanished.

He stopped walking and closed his eyes against the bitter rain, inhaling the invigorating, briny tang, allowing its chilly fluttering to dry his parted lips and fill his expectant lungs. As his thoughts gently ebbed away, all that remained were the soothing, lapping waves. A sharp tug pulled him back to the moment. Casting an abandoned glance downwards, he recognised his sodden yet eager companion. Managing a smile, he continued along the empty beach.

Tom had walked his dog every morning since the move and most evenings—weather permitting. Not that he needed or wanted the company, or that Scamp needed the exercise, it was simply another way he had learned to shroud his obsession of the sea, appearing as a normal, pet-walking nobody.

"Fetch!"

He watched Scamp dissolve into the vaporous obscurity while listening to the receding scrunch of inspirited footfalls as the sea breeze insisted on spinning the small bag he carried for the old man, containing simple refreshments. Tom desperately wished to know his story, he assumed it was a sad one, a story that could irrevocably alter a man's destiny and claim his mind. During the worst of the weather, Tom could still make out the old man's silhouette from his beach-front apartment window, sat slumped against the white concrete coastal wall, alone and staring out to sea.

For almost a year Tom had regularly walked this beach and although missing only a handful of days, he had never seen the destitute soul move from his spot. Quite often he would watch as others approached, either out of curiosity or to offer something by way of concern, only to leave confused and shrugging away the uncomfortable experience.

Tom had spoken to him previously on several occasions, but not once did he receive a coherent reply. The destitute man would only stare towards the mercurial, undulating lines that approached, crested upon dark emerald waves, ceaseless in their delivery. His vacant gaze would never wander below to the bubbly lace netting the tiny stones, or to the sliding tide that welcomed the solemn waves, each bowing in turn. Although nothing of substance had ever passed between them, Tom sensed something greater within himself, a deeper underlying sympathy that transcended charity, it felt worryingly personal and irrational.

He recalled his initial encounter, the only time he witnessed any significant change in the despondent man. He had knelt down and spoken to him, watching a single tear escape from his distant eyes, eyes that looked inexplicably familiar, as did his weather-beaten face, or at least what was not sunken beneath his feral beard. The old man seemed to be on the verge of uttering something, his shallow breath became forced and urgent.

Tom had leaned in further, then without warning a bitterly cold hand seized his own and the stranger managed to croak out a warning, “Let me see, it’s not your time, let me see!”

The sincerity in his words was alarming. Tom had tried to pull away, from his fetid, salty breath, his rheumy, watery eyes that mirrored the dark-green rolling waves, but was unable to unclasp his hand until the old man’s rasping had finally settled down.

From that moment on, Tom had realised his unreceptive manner was not born of arrogance and held genuine sympathy for his condition. He had gained some small measure of comfort in seeing the simple food he had been leaving appeared to be being eaten.

Where was his dog?

"Scamp!"

A discordant string of excited barks echoed back. Tom increased his pace and Scamp blurred back into view, barking at where the old man usually sat.

"Get away from him, Scamp!"

His dog reluctantly returned by his side, looking crestfallen and anxious. Tom was about to apologise until he realised he was looking only upon a discarded heap of wet clothes, surrounded by a few tattered plastic bags tied together, rustling noisily in the breeze. Scamp looked up for approval, then tottered off anyway to fossick further. Tom walked over to where Scamp was poking around and stared down at the deserted jumble.

So sad, what had happened to the old man? Perhaps he was finally taken into care? thought Tom.

As tragic as the stranger's tale may have been, his disappearance had hopefully signified an end to his pain and yet a melancholy so severe had suddenly seized Tom.

Rooted to the spot, he was unable to shift his gaze until Scamp's insistence directed his awareness to a glass bottle by his feet. Tom's heart immediately sank, while revulsion and panic smothered and tightened about him like a winter vine's embrace. The familiar object seemed to vibrate, triggering an instant release of ageless memories that pounded his mind. A fractured history embodying torment of impossible duration brought him to his knees.

Tom was oblivious to Scamp's sorrowful mix of whimpers and barks, sitting just feet away from his shaking body, yet oddly the intoxicating sound of the waves had never left him. Only now, the rhythmic wash had increased to a deafening roar, threatening to engulf him entirely.

Grasping the weathered glass bottle, he began to wail insufferably, swaying upon his drenched knees in the unforgiving shingle. Although weeping he could still determine two pieces of paper stuffed inside. Tom grappled with the cork stopper, his trembling fingers terrified to reveal what he already knew deep inside.

Removing the first scrap of paper he read the scrawled words, words that occasionally swelled as his earnest tears strove to erase them...

"I am so, so sorry, my boy, I really hoped we had done it this time.

I waited and never stopped watching. Towards the end I didn't even mind, I was just so happy to not see our cursed bottle for so long, but eventually, it found me again.

I wanted a different life for you, for us, a better one. One to end them all and end this madness.

We'll do it, we will, we'll reach her this time... "

Sobbing fiercely, Tom held himself, fearful he would completely unravel. His loathsome glare now fixed upon the second time-worn scrap of parchment. He removed it mechanically, feeling disassociated from his life and so utterly alone. He unrolled the parchment and remembered the ancient words instantly before he read them.

"Swim o'er to thy song, thy sweetest of Siren's calls,

She waits for thou, now and evermore,

Seek her out and diminish not your light,

Ne'er doubt nor cease, or thy cycle will ne'er be banished,

Godspeed, God bless."

Knowing what he must do, the young man stood and fastened the cork tightly after replacing only the old parchment back inside. Scamp watched his owner remove his clothes in silence. He placed his belongings inside one of the plastic bags and knelt down beside his dog.

"Good boy, stay here. Someone will find you, someone who will take better care of you. Please forgive me... " said Tom, squeezing Scamp tightly for the last time, feeling his small, damp body shake with cold and confusion.

Condemned; he carried the bottle towards the unchangeable waves, just as he had done countless times before. Tom barely noticed the bracing spume, rising and splashing as he walked, drawing him deeper into its inky dominion. After his head had submerged, he couldn't tell if the seabed had given way or he was still walking upon it, such was the numbness that had claimed his frozen body. Tom raised his hand—still grasping the bottle—and began to swim headlong against the crashing waves, unfaltering in their harshness.

Fighting to breathe it was all Tom could do to remain afloat, cleaving his arms into the murky onslaught that had denied him from his resolution, sanity or peace for an eternity.

"Where are you? What do you want from me? I hate you! I need you!"

In weary, reckless despair, Tom lost his grip upon the bottle. In a blind panic he flailed wildly in search of the only thing that could end his suffering yet also unpityingly prolong it. Wiping his stinging, teary eyes, he strained desperately to see anything between the dark rolling clouds and the relentless spray whipped up from the boisterous, curling swells.

When he believed all was but lost, he caught sight of the bottle bobbing wildly upon a surging wave and swam towards it, only to watch it become tossed farther away. He knew he was rapidly losing his strength, caught between saving the one thing he loathed above all else and the only thing that would finally bring his soul to rest. But without the bottle how could he ever warn himself he had failed in his quest again?

Tom launched towards the dipping capsule, his world becoming a froth-capped darkness of unfathomable cruelty, taunting his supreme efforts as he dragged himself forwards lost in fear and fury. Gasping from the impossible struggle, he finally claimed it back from the sea, then doggedly headed back into the obscure unknown once again.

Severely spent, Tom now entered a delirium. Becoming hypothermic from the frozen sea temperatures and from sheer exhaustion, his body was beginning to fail him. Infrequently, flashes of light would fill his vision accompanied by a flurry of countless images, images of former lives, all carrying their summation of intense sadness splintering his drifting mind, like floating shards of deadwood clashing in stormy waters.

He could have been swimming out to sea for a minute or for a day, what was time to him? Tom's arms eventually slowed, and his benumbed, heavy head sagged dangerously, until he caught a wondrous melody. It was the most beautiful sound he had ever heard in this life and struggled towards it despite his withering essence. His eyes, now indifferent to the stinging salty waters began to weep once again. His tears a plea of mercy to the lamenting tide that coaxed him, sinking further beneath with every beguiling trough he entered.

"Never... stop... searching."

Tom could now see a small island full of radiant light, its captivating brilliance compelling beyond anything he could have imagined! Perched upon a craggy rock, she sat, enticing, waiting for him, beckoning him ever closer. The Sirens song was pure and irresistible, drowning out the tempest he floundered within, offering but a mortal taste of something his spirit had craved for so long.

He was unbearably close, but so terribly exhausted. His frozen arms had finally stopped moving and Tom was unable to feel anything anywhere, but a dull ache flooding his sinking heart. In spluttering dismay he managed to turn around and face the distant shore. Scamp was now nowhere to be seen. All he could perceive was a tiny silhouette of someone sat looking out to sea.

Tom released the bottle towards the shore and watched it nod away, just like his reoccurring dream.

"Next time, I will reach her... " he vowed, again.

A PROBLEM SOLVED

By Catherine Wilson

Catherine shares some amusing incidents of her childhood

My mother said that a problem could always be solved by giving it some serious thought. In other words, diagnose the problem first. I believe I have unconsciously worked on that principal all my life. More often than not the end result worked. When it didn't, I was called a 'know all' and blamed. The results were disastrous, funny, or both, depending upon who was judging.

Many solutions were made up and worked. Some medical remedies were gleaned from the medical profession, and others from old wives; especially from ancient Granny Ford who lived in a cottage behind a sweet shop in the town; she was an angelic bookies runner, well known to the constabulary, and a mine of misinformation to anyone who would listen.

I listened well when I went to place bets for my foster mother on the way to infants' school. Granny gave me toffee, which I wasn't allowed, and information I didn't know I'd digested.

It was rumoured that every night, she used the locked-up washhouse at the end of the yard to boil up potions for everything. Once she gave me a disgusting spoonful of remedy to get my sums right, not my favourite subject, but it worked even if it was only for that one day.

I had a big splinter in my finger one morning.

"Come 'ere my love I'll have it out in a jiffy," she said.

I was squeamish and couldn't look as she prodded then squeezed. I howled. It hurt like hell, but in a few seconds it was out. I stared at the gaping hole in my finger, filled with blood. She smeared some brown gunge over it, with a strip of rag for a bandage.

"There you are my love, a nasty one that was," she said. "It could 've gone all septic if we'd left bits in."

I was wishing it had, but at lunchtime when I proudly took off the rag to show my friends the hole, there was not a trace. Surely, she really was a witch.

One of our houses had a brick outbuilding which we kids used as a den. There was an old paraffin stove on a shelf. We were older by now – at least aged ten and had been learning to make toffee at school. One of the girls suggested we made some of our own. Everyone brought a small amount of the ingredients; one of the boys supplied an old saucepan. Everything was ready, when we realized we had no paraffin – only the matches.

That's where my diagnostic ability came in. I knew where there was a bottle of methylated spirits and assured all eight of us it would work just as well. A boy was dispatched to get it.

Of course, it didn't work. Creeping transparent blue flames and waves of dense black smoke which coated everything – cobwebs, walls, and us. Choking, we got ourselves outside to the lawn where we rolled about laughing at the state of us all. Like a meeting of chimney sweeps.

The merriment didn't last long, as two screaming mothers arrived and dragged their kids home. No-one blamed me. I was the smallest.

My most famous 'know it all' disaster was much later. I had a new job at a children's charity which had just moved to a large old converted workhouse surrounded by smaller homes throughout the grounds. It was Christmas time. When we found the lights, which were normal light bulbs painted and joined together on the flex, they wouldn't reach across the room. No problem for 'know all' here.

"Just cut the wires on one, and make sure the colour is twisted to its matching one on the other."

"Are you sure?" the Matron asked.

I assured her I'd watched my Dad do it at home.

We all had a go and held them up for the children to see how long it was. They clapped excitedly. The staff stood around the room with them as Matron got ready to do the big switch on.

The lights went out with a violent crash and sparks. Matron kept her cool and shouted for everyone to stand still, I had a feeling she'd half expected it.

"It's only the fuse," she said taking a torch from her apron pocket and glaring at me. It wasn't. I had cleverly fused the whole building – and the other homes dotted around the grounds which were on the same circuit.

I only vaguely remember the chaos of the next eight or ten hours. Not the best image as a new employee!

MY FAVOURITE THING

By Marilyn Pemberton

I love the weight of a book on my lap,
Heavy with words and their meaning.
Tales of romance for those who still hope;
Stories of crime for those too fearful to act.

Books have always been a part of my life,
At table we girls were allowed to read,
Father preferring the rustle of pages
To the chatter of daughters three.

No television then to entertain,
Instead Enid Blyton enthralled.
Oh! To be one of the Famous Five,
Or to travel to distant lands on a Wishing Chair.

I have always had a book lying around,
To be picked up and enjoyed at any time.
To take the opportunity for just a while
To escape real life into the world inside.

To me the only decoration a room needs,
Is a bookcase full of colourful spines,
That draws one's fingers like a magnet,
To see what is imprisoned within.

The best are the books from Victorian times,
That smell of dust and ages past,
With dedications written lovingly in copperplate
To a beneficiary who is no longer even a memory.

These days my library fits in my pocket,
On a device just six by four.
My favourite thing?
A Kindle of course.

EVERY BREATH

By Maxine Burns

The expression on a shopper's face inspired Maxine to write this story.

In a few seconds I'll be out of sight, just a few more steps. I breathe out hard. How long can you hold your breath? The sensation of being watched switches off, as if there's been a power cut. The relief is so powerful I feel dizzy and lean against the supermarket door.

I glance at my watch. I've got twenty minutes, tops, so I hurry to the trolley park, grab one and look at my shopping list. Only the usual mundane goods, baked beans, white sliced. Nothing nice, or different or tasty. I would love to be able to take time, browse, buy treats for Chloe, some sweets or perhaps a comic.

I sprint to the tinned goods aisle and gallop along, as if I'm taking part in a trolley dash. I grab a four pack of beans, then put them back. I'll be able to return sooner if I take less. Strawberry jam. He hasn't specified the brand he wants. I know he doesn't like the cheaper products, but it's nearing the end of the month and he's moaning about money. How much we cost him. If I get it wrong, I'll be in trouble.

I take a breath, chuck a mid-priced jar in the trolley and move on. Milk, tea, squash, a local paper. I pause for a few seconds to caress the lovely display of flowers. I bought some once, only a cheap bunch of daffs, but he was furious and locked Chloe in her room for two days. She wasn't allowed food and it was terrible listening to her cries, to know he was punishing her for my mistake. I'm thinking of killing him. I'm thinking it's the only way out. I have to look for an opportunity, because I'll only get one chance. But I'll have to act soon. Before he kills me. Before he kills Chloe.

I pay. I have the exact amount of money for the shopping. The beans were on offer and I get 25p change. He'll want the receipt, so I make sure I don't forget it.

I'm done.

I have four minutes before he'll expect to see me, and I take a seat in the customer café. I can't afford a coffee but no one seems to mind. I like to watch the shoppers. A few are laughing, holding hands. Some, like me, are alone. All shapes and sizes and ages. All leading normal lives. All free.

I take the mobile phone from my pocket, pray he hasn't noticed it's missing and scroll down the names. Well, that doesn't take very long. There are only two, the doctor and my mother. He doesn't allow me to have friends. I long to call my mum and press my fingers lightly over the numbers. I can't do more than that. She can't help me, and he will check the phone, see what I have done.

You see, he has Chloe in the house, with him. He really doesn't need to watch for me through binoculars, or to hit me if I'm late home, or if I have the wrong product, or if he feels like it. She's the thread that pulls me back. If I'm late, he'll hurt her. If I don't return, he'll kill her. So, I die instead, a little bit, every day we spend with him.

I grab the shopping and leave the safety of the supermarket, cross the road and I'm back in his sights. As I approach the house I look up to the bedroom. I can feel his binoculars trained on me, and the glass glints in the sunlight. The bags feel heavier with each step, my shoulder cramps.

A woman is walking toward me. She has a little dog on a red tartan lead. She smiles, and I lower my eyes. He'll think I'm speaking to her. I wish Chloe could have a little dog with a smart lead.

He is watching as I approach the door, I can see his outline through the frosted glass, still as death, waiting.

There is a commotion behind me. Someone is shouting and I look round. Oh my God! It's the woman, the little dog, she is waving at me, shouting, 'Hey.'

My insides freeze, I'm going to vomit, right here on the street, right here on the pavement. I see him bolt up the stairs. Then, her hand is on my shoulder and I turn to look at her. She steps back. She sees the shock on my face, she smells my terror.

"Sorry," she says. "Are you okay? You've dropped this."

I look at the phone in her hand, it has fallen from my pocket. I moan and snatch it. I don't look at her. I don't thank her. My heart is beating so hard, I can't get the words out. I hurry up the path, to the house and open the door. I turn and look at her. She is staring, a worried, puzzled look on her face. I nod. Time stops, then she raises a hand, a farewell.

I close the door and hear the sound of heavy, angry boots stomping down the stairs.

HOOKED

By Bec Woods

A class exercises playing a game of Consequences led Bec to write this story.

"So, Charlie Watts, will you marry me?"

Ruby Chandler, the voluptuous red-haired Amazonian looked down at the subject of her question.

Charlie, slack-jawed and wide-eyed felt like he'd been felled by one of his opponents in the ring.

Though he hadn't seen it coming, the signs had been there right from the moment he laid eyes on her, bare naked and lounging on a blue velvet chaise-longue, suggestively eating strawberries.

Why didn't I sign up to the 'Cooking for the cack-handed' class he thought, instead of life drawing. But he knew why, he wanted to become cultured like Chris Eubank, escape the Neanderthal tag that came with his profession.

"Well?" Ruby's green eyes penetrated Charlie's black, bloodshot ones. Her lips pouted in a fulsome bud of red lipstick, drawing him in, threatening to devour him like the strawberries that she loved to eat.

He couldn't look at a strawberry now without thinking of her and felt that the tiny seeds that adorned each piece of fruit were extensions of her eyes, all seeing, all knowing. He had nightmares about them – him landing in a strawberry patch after receiving a glancing blow from an opponent; not being able to get up and being counted out by the referee.

"Perhaps you need a little sweetener," Ruby leaned in, her chest threatening to suffocate Charlie.

Charlie leaned back, even when he was up against the ropes in a fight, there always seemed to be a way out.

A respite was granted as Ruby disappeared into the kitchen. But when she returned with a round cake tin, he knew his fate was sealed.

He watched helplessly as Ruby slowly eased a home-made Victoria sponge from the tin.

"Knock out," said Charlie.

"So that's a yes?" said Ruby.

THE KING AND I

by Margaret Mather

Inspired by the King himself, Margaret has written about the little-known time when Elvis visited England.

Most people believe that Elvis only ever visited the UK once. That was when he touched down at Prestwick Airport to change planes. Not true, no siree. He also appeared at the Lime Tree Park Working Men's club in Coventry. How did that come about you may ask? Well it all happened through Elvis's friendship with Larry Grayson.

Elvis had known of Larry for a few years. He was a huge fan of Larry's Saturday evening television programme called *'Shut that Door'.* When he heard that Larry was coming to Las Vegas he invited him backstage. They hit it off in a big way and became firm friends. Larry would always stay at *Gracelands* when he was anywhere near Memphis and Elvis was grateful to Larry for all his help and advice.

One day while warming up for a performance at the *Hilton* in Las Vegas, Elvis had a call from Larry.

"Hey Elvis, how are you?" asked Larry.

"Hey man, just great. You OK?"

"Yes, well I would be if this stupid man who I had lined up to sing in my show, hadn't broken his leg. I don't suppose you could come over and fill the gap? I know its short notice, but it would be great to see you. "

Elvis thought for a moment and decided that yes, he would do it. Larry was a friend and the inspiration for some of his biggest hits. Songs like *'Jailhouse Rock'*, inspired by Larry's famous catch phrase – *'Shut that door'*. Then there was *'Heartbreak Hotel'*, which took its inspiration from another of Larry's much-loved catch phrases – *'Oh I say, look at the muck in here'*. And of course, Larry's fictional character, 'Slack Alice', was inspirational in one of his much-loved hits – *'That's The Wonder Of You'*. Another character was *'Pop-it-in-Pete – the postman'*, and yes, you've guessed it – *'Return to Sender'*. How could he possibly refuse?

"OK man, I do have a free week next week and I would love to see you again. One condition though."

"Anything Elvis, anything your little wooden heart desires."

"I want to appear in disguise. All the women in the USA want me to perform in my black leathers, but I'm fed up with screaming women running behind me. They try to grab me in some crazy places. Some have scissors and want to cut off my clothes or my hair. I can tell you man it's real scary at times."

"Elvis, that's awful. That would be my worst nightmare, women trying to undress me."

"Here's the deal then, Larry. If you can arrange a good disguise for me, then I'll come over and perform in your show. How does that grab you, man?"

"Consider it done. There's a costume hire shop in Coventry. I'll arrange everything. I can't wait to see you again. Thanks, Elvis."

"It's a pleasure, man, after all what are friends for?"

Larry was like a dog with two tails. He arranged the hire of the costume and had posters printed which said:

ELVIS LOOK-ALIKE SHOW AT LIME TREE PARK
WORKING MENS CLUB.
SATURDAY NIGHT – MISS IT AND YOU'LL BE – ALL
SHOOK UP! AHA HA!

The big day finally arrived. Larry along with his friend Everard, (yes, he was real), waited at Birmingham Airport. They could hardly contain their excitement. Elvis came out of the arrival's hall looking like an extra from Oklahoma. He was wearing a cowboy hat, white cowboy boots, blue jeans, a red checked shirt and sunglasses. Larry thought that he stood out like a sore thumb but what the heck, no one seemed to recognise him.

"Elvis, over here" shouted Larry in his excitement, totally forgetting that Elvis didn't want to be recognised.

People turned to look but when they saw Larry they thought, 'It's only Larry fooling around.'

"That was close; I nearly gave the game away, sorry Elvis."

"No problem, man, no one recognised me."

They all piled into Everard's mini and headed for Larry's house.

"Nice pad, Larry. I love your record collection and is that a juke box over there? I'll have a closer look tomorrow. Better go and catch some shut eye so that I'll be ready to rock and roll tonight. How many people will be there tonight – five, six thousand?"

"No Elvis, not that many." Larry thought it best not to elaborate. "Now, when you wake up, I'll take you to Coventry for a meal before the show."

"Can we have some fish and chips? I've heard a lot about English fish and chips."

"Of course, we can. We'll get fish, chips and mushy peas from Fishy Moore's in town."

Elvis was too tired to ask what mushy peas were.

When he woke up, they made their way to Coventry. The fish, chips and mushy peas went down a treat. They then carried on to the club. It wasn't as big as Elvis had expected however he never said anything to Larry. The stage was small, and Elvis did ask how the band would all fit on the stage, to which Larry replied,

"Sorry, Elvis, no band, just you, your guitar and a backing track."

Better and better, thought Elvis.

Larry handed Elvis a bag with his costume in and Elvis changed in the toilets because there were no changing rooms.

"Hey, Larry, where did you get this outfit?" Elvis shouted over the top of the toilet door. I really like it, man. I think I'll have some made for my shows back home."

Elvis emerged in a white all-in-one suit, covered in millions of sparkling rhinestones and sequins, a black plastic wig, a cape lined with the red, white and blue of the American flag, and a pair of sunglasses with black fur sideburns attached.

"Oh, Elvis." Larry gasped. "You look stunning, do you like it?"

"It's mighty fine, Larry, mighty fine. It's much better than a black leather skin-tight suit. Thanks Larry."

Elvis went on stage and belted out some of his biggest hits. He did expect more than 150 people in the room, and he wasn't used to the way people spoke to each other during his performance. He was also upset when a committee man switched his microphone off half-way through 'Love Me Tender' to announce:

"If anyone wants more drinks, then get them now while the act is on. No one will get served at the bar when the bingo starts and there will be no talking during the bingo. You have five minutes."

Then turning to Elvis, he said, "Carry on lad, you're doing a grand job. One of my favourite songs that."

The second half went well with no more interruptions. Elvis sang his heart out.

In the audience sat Flo with a packet of pork scratchings and a glass of brown ale. She turned to her friend Maude and said, "He can fairly wiggle those hips and belt out a good song but he's nothing like the real thing."

Sadly, Elvis never came back to the UK. He thought that our clubs would be bigger and audiences not so rude, and mushy peas – you could keep them. They didn't agree with his digestive system.

However, he did adopt the rhinestone jumpsuit and until the day he died that was all he ever wore at concerts.

A GAME OF KINGS

By Marilyn Pemberton

Wandering past an antiques shop, Marilyn spotted a chess set...

A shop selling the past; artefacts once loved but now abandoned.
Ornaments grimy and chipped, fabrics faded and forlorn.
I am drawn to a corner, hidden in dusty shadows.
Nothing there but an excess of the unwanted.
Nothing there, but still something pulls and I see a Queen,
Smiling a smile of invitation.
She fits in the palm of my hand and is blood warm.
I blow off the motes of the years to reveal a gown of white and a crown of gold.

Back home I clean each miniature with care,
Each is intricate and individual,
Each painted expression warm and benign
Except that of the black King, who frowns and glowers.
I place each piece on black or white ebony,
Their realm protected by a frame of carved ivory;
Serpents entwined around stems with exotic blooms and deadly thorns,
Malefic devils peeping round corners, leering and lascivious.

The dying sun casts its last rays
Lighting up the white army so that it glows,
Radiating purity and amity.
The black ranks lurk in the shadows,
Exuding ill will and malice.

I idly move a white pawn forward,
Admiring the detail of his cavalry uniform,
Admiring the determined set of his chin.

Night falls and I discover there is no power
And so resort to candles.
The shadows perform a tribal dance on the walls
And the smell of vanilla permeates the air.
A makeshift supper then a book,
The words barely discernible in the romantic glow.
Eyes heavy I stand to leave but stop dead,
A black pawn has broken rank.

I try to return him to his rightful place,
But he is as stubborn as his obdurate expression.
Surely his sabre was in his scabbard before
And not thrust out with such aggression?
Is it the candle flame that flickers,
Or a wave of disquiet that ripples through the white ranks?
No black will move under my touch
Only another white pawn, hesitant and fearful.

I watch and watch.
But the pieces move in my imagination only.
I watch and watch, not knowing what for.
The flames become erratic in their death throes,
Then absolute darkness.
I watch and watch yet hear nothing.
But the rays of the re-born sun reveal a black knight positioned for battle,
And my blood runs cold in my veins.

The outside recedes into infinity

And my world is reduced to a square of squares.
I feel no hunger for food nor thirst for water
But have an appetite for a fight.
I move my rider into battle,
Reluctant though he seems.
The white side lets out a sigh
The black side lets out a roar.

I sit transfixed, unblinking.
And before my very eyes a black pawn slides across a square,
As silent as death.
And before my very eyes he raises his sabre into the air,
As silent as death.
His eyes are black pools of hatred turned on me;
His grin is not one of merriment but of malevolence.
I sit transfixed, unblinking.

I am an unskilled player at best
And I am not at my best.
I know I have erred when my man looks at me in horror
Moments before he is slain.
The white of his jacket turns red
And he slides off the board and lies limp, yes limp.
I touch him and feel the warmth turn to ice cold,
As cold as the blood that runs through my veins.

The sun sears its arc in the sky again and again;
When I relight the tapers the shadows are now still, transfixed,
Watching the game.
Each loss of my own drains me, as each loss of my foe revives me.
I yearn for nothing but to win,

And am exultant when my bishop beheads his rival
In a move that leaves a red stain that I cannot shift.
And still the shadows sit and watch, transfixed.

I have no concept of time.
Have I been fighting for a day, a month, a lifetime?
The pile of dead grows and grows,
The blood dripping onto the carpet,
Each drop reverberating like a clash of cymbals,
Drip, drip, clash.
My head pounds, my hands shake
But I am still in the game.

Each move is such an effort now,
My energy is seeping from me
As the blood is seeping from the fallen.
I fear to move any piece in case it is his last;
I cannot bear to hear the anguished cries.
The blacks strain forwards in impatience,
The whites cringe back in dread.
I am frozen with indecision.

There is a pounding in my ears,
Not the pulsing of my own blood,
But the stamping of tiny feet.
Pound, pound, pound.
The sound is insistent, demanding, unrelenting.
Pound, pound, pound.
The black King throws back his head and out of his black mouth
Comes a war cry that freezes the blood in my veins.

In my panic I make a move,

And to my horror see the black Queen slide triumphantly across the board
Towards my own niveus Regina,
Who lifts her head bravely to bare her white throat,
For the blade that slices.
And she sighs my name.
And the remnants of my pathetic army let out a wail of despair;
A requiem for the death of their Queen and of their hope.

I know I cannot win.
I have lost the will to fight,
I have lost the will to live.
There is only one move left.
My King gives me a look as courageous as I have ever seen,
And I knock him over gently;
Surrendering the game, surrendering the fight,
Surrendering my life.

As he falls so do I.
Our eyes lock and we witness each other's demise.
There is no sound but the gloating cries of jubilation
That rebound off the walls and inside my skull.
I see the leering grin of the black King
As he plunges his sword into the heart of his opponent,
And into my own.
As the white King's eyes close, so do mine.

I should be dead.
I would be dead if a dear friend
In his concern at my evasion
Had not broken down the door.
He says my cry had rent the air like the howl of a banshee,

But my cry only.
He cannot hear the shouts of victory
And the wails of defeat.

He has saved my life but my life is still forfeit.
My strength does not return,
I sleep only in snatches.
The blood runs cold in my veins
So that I shiver like one with the ague.
And my face remains as white as snow, as white as a sheet,
As white as the gown of my dear Queen,
Whose voice I hear, calling me.

The night times are the worst.
I hear the pounding of the drums
And the pounding of feet
And the pounding of hooves
On the attic floor above.
And the sigh of the sword,
And the sigh of her breath
As she calls my name.

I know that they are waiting,
Waiting for me to play again.
I have no life,
But I fear death.
I know I will get no peace,
No rest,
Until I play their game,
The game of Kings.

STRANGER IN THE PARK

By Ella Cook

This story has been written as a thank you and comes with the following message: "With heartfelt thanks to the real-life 'Ethan'. You know who you are, and you've changed my life for the better. Thank you."

The last few steps had stolen almost everything that had been left of her dwindling energy. Exhausted she collapsed on the tree stump near the park gate.

Her bare fingers traced across the dry, tired wood. Somewhere, deep inside, she knew she should feel sad that this was all that was left of the great horse chestnut tree that had stood for so many years – supplying happy children with thousands of glossy brown conkers and hours of fun. She'd smashed dozens of conkers one year with a perfectly shaped brown wedge found under the branches that would have sheltered her if she'd sat in this very spot just a few months ago.

She knew she should feel something for the loss, but she just couldn't find the energy. It didn't really matter. Not much did.

The sadness engulfed her again, choking and all consuming. It left no room for anything else. It sucked all joy and hope and energy from her, leaving her a cold and dark shell. So cold that she couldn't feel the dampness that crept through her jeans from what remained of the once bright and strong tree. The first frostiness of autumn didn't even make her shiver.

Her throat tightened painfully, and misery burnt in her eyes before streaming unheeded down her cheeks. But the tears didn't help or offer any respite. Nothing did.

She had no words to explain where it came from – the soul sucking sadness and worry that drained her every day and stole all the colour, joy and light from her life. Yes, she knew there was stress in her life, but other people had similar struggles and worries and seemed to handle them without collapsing in on themselves.

When she had more energy, she would sometimes try to force herself to think about it logically – and every time she came to the same conclusion: there was no real reason for her to feel so rotten, and damaged and hopeless. Which often made her feel even worse.

Blinded by tears which she couldn't understand, she didn't notice the strange man until he was a few feet in front of her, kneeling to rummage through the autumn leaves. She stared at him dully, aware she should be reacting to the presence of a stranger who seemingly had little regard for personal space, but not caring enough to do anything about it.

As if reading her thoughts, he looked up with an apologetic smile. "Sorry, but this one was too beautiful to resist." He held up a gloved hand to show her his treasure – a dark, glossy conker nestling in his palm amongst bits of dried leaves.

"It's fine." She snuffled, not caring.

"Doesn't look that fine." He slipped the conker into a pocket and produced a neatly folded handkerchief instead.

She stared blankly at the white fabric shoved under her nose.

"Please."

She wasn't sure if it was a question, or a command, but she didn't want to have to make the effort to make polite conversation with anyone. Least of all a stranger. And she didn't have the energy to argue. So, she slowly grasped the handkerchief in stiff fingers and patted it ineffectively against her cheeks before trying to hand it back to him, hoping he would take the hint and leave her alone with her misery.

"You look like you might be needing it for a bit longer. You should hold onto it." He gave her gave her a reassuring smile. "I've got a few errands to run. I won't be long. Maybe you will want to share your problems and try halving them when I get back. If you're still here."

She shrugged, not knowing what she wanted to do. "I wouldn't bother if I were you."

He echoed her gesture. "Well you're not me, and it's not a bother. Your choice whether you will be here or not." He patted her shoulder before sauntering towards the gate, hands tucked tightly in his pockets against the cold.

She stared at her shoulder, surprised at the warmth that still lingered from his brief touch. When she looked up, he'd vanished from sight. Her eyes fell to the bright white cloth twisted between her fingers, providing stark contrast with her abused skin, already overly pink from the cold. She twisted it more tightly around her fingers, watching as they swelled and darkened from the pressure before flushing back to a healthy colour. She released the knot she'd twisted.

She did it again and again, wishing there was a similar release valve she could find for her own mind.

As usual, time was fickle. When she wanted it to rush by, it seemed guaranteed to drag, and yet weekends and evenings seemed to vanish in a few blinks, forcing her to paste her mask and smile back on and pretend normality again. Now, it raced by and disappeared in a whirl, and she heard frosty leaves crunch to a stop beside her.

"Guess maybe you fancy that walk then."

For the first time she looked at him properly and bothered to take in his features. Mousey blond hair stuck out askew from a yellow, hand knitted hat that sat above kind blue eyes that peered down at her, framed by a few wrinkles. She struggled to determine his age. He could have been a younger man who'd had a hard life, or an older one who was just ageing well. Average height, average build, average hair, average clothes. There was nothing that stood out about him. Except that he'd now stopped to talk to her, a total stranger, twice.

She knew she should have headed home when she'd had the chance. But now that he was standing beside her, rocking back on his feet as he waited for her response, she felt it would be too rude to run away. And she didn't have the energy to make excuses.

"I'm going to wander round the edge of the park. You should walk with me. It's pretty cold to be staying still today."

She watched as he sauntered off slowly and gnawed on her lip. The sensible thing would be to stand up and head home, and maybe find something to eat. She forced herself to stand, but instead of trudging back towards the gate, her traitorous feet quick-stepped after him as if compelled by some unknown force.

He smiled as she drew level with him, and they fell into an easy pace. Neither spoke as they slowly followed the winding path around the park, but she felt the grim weight slowly begin to ease from her shoulders as they circumvented one corner, and then another. By the time the gate had meandered back into view, they had barely spoken, but she felt lighter than she had done in weeks.

She hesitated when they reached the gate and held out the handkerchief, suddenly oddly reluctant to relinquish her grip on it, and unsure of what to do.

He made it easy for her, gently pushing the white cloth into her hand and folding her fingers over it. "I'll probably be here next week, around the same time. If you fancied another walk."

"Maybe." She shrugged non-committedly.

"No pressure. Just letting you know my plans." He turned back after a few steps. "I'm Ethan by the way."

"Norah."

"Nice to meet you, Norah. I hope you have a good week." Sincerity shone from his eyes for a few moments, before he turned on his heel and headed back the way he had come, hands jammed deeply in his pockets.

For the whole week Norah had convinced herself that the last place she was going to be was in the park again, but when the morning rolled around, she found herself hovering anxiously by the gate. It hadn't been one of her best weeks, and she'd spent a lot of it with her head buried under the duvet, feeling heart breakingly miserable and not fully understanding why. She'd avoided the phone and social media, unable to summon the energy to pretend to be OK. Maybe that was why she'd forced herself out of bed and into clothes this morning. Because he had offered her company without asking anything of her.

She'd just about convinced herself that, of course, Ethan wasn't going to show up and that she should just go home and go back to bed when familiar footsteps crunched up the path behind her.

She let out a breath that she hadn't even realised she'd been holding and felt her shoulders relax a little.

"Hey Norah," he gave her an easy smile as he swung the gate open. "How's your week been?"

"OK," Norah lied automatically as they fell into step.

"Really?" Ethan shot her a quizzical look.

Norah's mask melted away under the honesty of his gaze. "Well, maybe a little less than OK. Pretty shit really."

"I can listen while we walk."

"I don't know." Norah hesitated.

"Why not?" His breath puffed in the cold air. "Have somewhere else to be? Something more important to do?"

"No, not really," Norah admitted quietly. "But why would you want to listen to my problems?"

Ethan shrugged. "I'm going for a walk anyway. If inviting you to walk with me and share whatever's worrying you can improve your day, why shouldn't I do that?"

"I... don't know. When you put it like that, it sounds so simple."

"It is simple." Ethan smiled at her. "You'll talk, I'll listen, and we'll both walk."

"I don't know where to start." Norah fell into step beside him.

"Some people say the beginning is a good place."

"And what if you don't know where it all started?"

"Well, I guess you could tell me why you were sitting on a cold tree stump, if you wanted to," Ethan offered carefully.

Norah took a deep breath, trying to find the words to explain feelings she was still struggling to understand herself. He waited patiently, and eventually she began to speak, letting the emotions trip off her tongue, releasing some of their poison into the air like the puffs of breath they escaped on.

And as promised, while she talked, he listened, and they both walked.

The golden reds of autumn faded, extinguished by the bitter greys and crystalline whites of winter, and still he was there every week – wearing the same battered yellow hat and fingerless gloves as the first day she'd met him. They walked the same path, and every week it became less of a trudge for Norah as her mood and steps lightened.

As winter blossomed into spring, Norah found herself coming back to life. Challenges seemed less insurmountable and the things that had worried her so much in the past were much easier to manage. She was making plans, spending time with friends, and doing well at work. She was enjoying life again and starting to feel happy again. And it was all because of him.

She waved cheerfully as Ethan approached.

"Hey Norah, how's your week been?"

"Good thanks," she smiled happily. "There's been a lot going on still, but I'm managing it and still feeling pretty happy."

"I'm glad to hear that." Ethan hesitated. "There's something I need to talk to you about."

"Of course," Norah nodded, eager to learn more about her mysterious friend.

"I'm afraid this is the last week we'll be able to meet." He turned to look at Norah, whose feet were frozen to the floor. "Don't look so worried. Come on, keep walking and talking."

She fell into their regular pattern without thinking. "Where are you going? Is it work?"

"You could say that." He watched her try to process the news. "Keep talking, Norah."

She took a deep breath and let the words tumble from her tongue. "I'm scared. You've helped me so much, and now you're leaving." Panic edged her voice. "I don't know how I'm going to do this without you."

"You're fine, Norah. You don't need me anymore. Look at you, you're happy now."

"Maybe now. But what happens when something goes wrong? How will I cope?"

"You'll cope by being you," Ethan reassured her. "You're ready for this Norah, you have been for weeks now, and you know that."

"But..." Norah's argument trailed off as she realised he was right. "But I like knowing you're here."

"I know. But you don't need me, and that's the point. You're going to be fine, Norah. Better than fine... you're going to thrive and excel and be happy."

Norah shook her head. "I wish I could be as sure as you are."

"I think you are," Ethan challenged, a smile in his eyes. "I think once you let yourself stop being scared, you do know this – and have done for some time."

Norah nodded, suddenly choked by emotion. "I don't know how to repay you. To thank you for your kindness." She'd never seen him anywhere except for the park, and knew that once she stepped through the gate, she'd likely never see him again.

"You don't need to."

"But I feel like I should." Norah argued, her steps slowing as the gate that signalled the end of their final walk came into view.

"It really isn't necessary." Ethan carried on walking at their normal pace, forcing her to catch up.

"I know you don't really talk about yourself, but will you answer one question?"

"If I can."

"Why did you stop to help me all those months ago? Why have you given me so much of your time?"

Ethan shrugged and answered easily. "Because you needed it, and because I could."

Ethan smiled as he watched her leave. Norah would be just fine – he knew that as strongly as he knew the sun would rise in the morning. He sauntered over to the tree stump where he had first met her so many months, and so many conversations, ago. After circling the stump twice, he decided on the spot he wanted. Reaching into his pocket, he produced a glossy, rich conker, and polished it against his trouser leg.

Kneeling down, he tucked it into the roots of its mother tree. He rested his hand over the flicker of life and closed his eyes as he called on a power far greater than his. Warmth flickered through him, and his palm glowed briefly with power.

After a few seconds he uncurled his fingers and smiled at the tiny green shoots that now wove their way through the brittle roots.

"Thank you." He looked at the sky, once again breath taken by the stunning pinks and golds that bid farewell to the day and welcomed the dusk.

After gifting himself a few moments to enjoy the beauty of the place one last time, he reached out his hand to catch a piece of paper that flirted with the breeze. He read the few lines curling across the paper and nodded once. "Of course."

Hidden by the golden light of dusk he took a few running steps, and leaped into the air, his wings unfurling and catching him before he hit the ground. The gentle thump of his wings matched the beat of his heart as he pushed through the air, racing to meet his next stranger in a park.

MEET THE AUTHORS

ANN EVANS

Ann began writing as a hobby when her children were little. It was a hobby that became a career. She has 32 books published to date, writing for children, young adults, reluctant readers, romance and thrillers; she also has well over 1,500 magazine articles published on a wide variety of topics. She's a former Feature Writer for the Coventry Telegraph. She's also a member of the Society of Women Writers' & Journalists, The Romantic Novelists' Association, The Crime Writers' Association, the National Association of Writers in Education and the Coventry Writers' Group.

Website: www.annevansbooks.co.uk
Facebook: www.facebook.com/Ann-Evans-Books
Twitter: www.twitter.com/annevansauthor
Blog: http://annsawriter.blogspot.com/

ALEX BARTLETT

Last year Alex's wife started disappearing into the cold dark nights. Bored of being left with the washing up – he decided to follow her and discovered that the mysterious "Wordsmiths" were warm and welcoming writers – who usually had cake. Lured in by the promise of baked goods and laugher he re-discovered his love of writing and is currently racing his wife to publication.

MAXINE BURNS

Maxine writes articles, short fiction, plays and poetry. Her published work includes having a play performed at the Blue/Orange Theatre, in Birmingham and was a winner in the Coventry Peace Festival poetry competition. She is presently working on a novel about a village populated by dark, dysfunctional families. Maxine is a member of The Women Writers and Journalists (SWWJ) and was Chair of The Coventry Writers Group for three years.

ELLA COOK

Ella's been obsessed with books since she was a toddler. She decided to become a writer as soon as she realised that stringing letters together in the right order could actually be a career. Since then, writing fiction has mostly been a hobby fitted around 'real life', but Ella has found time for a few short stories (one of which won the Coventry Writers Group trophy for 2018), and a couple of novels which she is still lovingly polishing before letting them escape into the big, wide world.

She grew up in the outskirts of London, where fairies lived at the bottom of her Grandma's garden, so it isn't surprising that she still looks for magic in everyday life – and often finds it.

When she's not living in a fantasy world of her own creation, she writes bids and develops programmes for children's services. She lives in rural Warwickshire (where there are probably more fairies) with her husband who is ever loving and understanding and makes her gallons of tea in magical cups that can keep drinks warm for whole chapters. He's also recently crashed her writing group and is featured in this anthology. Cheeky bugger ☺
You can contact Ella at ella.cook@hotmail.com

MARK HOWLAND

M. A. Howland is a rising fantasy author who lives in Warwickshire, UK, home to the great William Shakespeare and Mary Ann Evans. Originally studying at university for a Business Degree, Mark left prematurely at a tender age to join the military to seek out his adventure. After years of frustrating his commanding officers with his *philosophical* outlook, it was mutually agreed he should leave and pursue something of a more independent nature, other than just following orders. So, he became married and now lives happily with his wife, four little inspirations and an insane shorkie; still taking orders. The author is regularly active in the conservation of woodland and wildlife. He is also studying for his Bardship with OBOD (Order of Bards, Ovates, and Druids), due to his lifelong fascination of Druidry and ancient folklore, which by his own admission provides plenty of inspiration for his writing.

"I am fascinated by ancient folklore and in anything that is suspended outside of what we term the natural state. This is where you will find those illusive, magical creatures I feel so lovingly compelled to write about. I am also an advocate of wildlife and woodland preservation. For where would the Goblins roam without such a mystical place... your home?"
www.mahowland.com

MARGARET MATHER

Margaret grew up in Scotland and at 17 went to work as an au-pair in Norway. She moved to Coventry in 1971. She later worked as a typist in the export department of British Leyland and then in the offices of Glass Coventry. She then changed career and moved into the transport industry as a

Business Development Manager and worked for various distribution companies. She then became self-employed until her retirement in January 2013. She began writing around 30 years ago but due to work commitments it was only ever a hobby. Since retiring she has had more time to devote to her writing which has resulted in published short stories, articles and poems.

MARY OGILVIE

Mary is a long-standing member of the Coventry Writers' Group and has contributed towards the anthologies published by them over the years. She was also a Grassroots reporter on the Coventry Evening Telegraph reporting on local news in her area. Over the years Mary has written poetry, articles and short stories, some of which has been published.

MARILYN PEMBERTON

Marilyn is an IT Project Manager who started writing late in life. She gained her BA, MA & PhD as a part-time mature student and it was whilst researching Victorian fairy tales for her PhD that she came across a little-known writer called Mary De Morgan. Absolutely fascinated by this writer, Marilyn continued finding out as much as she could about her and in 2012, she *published Out of the Shadows: The Life and Works of Mary De Morgan.* (Cambridge Scholars Publishing).

By this time Marilyn had caught the writing bug and because there is still so little known about De Morgan, she decided to try to write a novel about the writer's life, using her imagination to fill in the gaps. This led to her publishing

The Jewel Garden. Her latest novel, *Song of the Nightingale* is due for publication in 2020. (Conrad Press). Novel three is in progress. None of these books would have happened if she had not attended Ann Evan's Monday Wordsmith writing group.
Website: https://marilynpemberton.wixsite.com/author
Blog: writingtokeepsane.wordpress.com

JACKIE SKIPP

Jackie only began writing seriously a few years ago, following a major illness. in November 2017 she started writing her first novel which she hopes to get published soon. She also writes short stories and poetry and has recently become a blogger for Warwickshire Year of Wellbeing. Jackie has led a busy life, bringing up four daughters and taking on a wide variety of jobs. She is currently a Wellbeing Co-ordinator but will shortly be taking on a new challenge as an NHS funded Senior Link Worker, introducing social prescribing into local primary care networks. She is determined that no matter how busy she becomes she won't stop writing.

ROBERT TYSALL

Rob was born and brought up in Rugby, Warwickshire, and played the sport the town is famous for in his youth, until he discovered a passion and talent for music and photography. His career so far has been a busy mix of being lead vocalist and percussionist in bands, playing as far afield as Bahrain in the Middle East; plus working as a professional freelance photographer. He is currently in a 60s, 70s & Beatles duo, and lives in Warwickshire with his wife, Heather. He has two grown up children who have

both followed in his footsteps with their musical talents. Rob is multi published on the photographic side of things with countless magazine articles published, having worked with writer Ann Evans for many years as a writer/photographer duo. For quite some time he has dabbled with the idea of writing a novel – a dream which has finally come to fruition as he and Ann teamed up to collaborate on a supernatural thriller which was published by Bloodhound Books in 2018. Now that he has been bitten by the writing bug, there's no stopping him, and two more book collaborations are currently in the pipeline.
http://www.tysallsphotogrpahy.org.uk
https://www.facebook.com/robert.tysall
https://twitter.com/TYSALLSPHOTOS

CATHERINE WILSON
Catherine has loved writing ever since she was a little girl of 10 or 11. Her career however took her into nursing, training at Gulson Hospital in Coventry and then going onto work in hospitals in Leamington and Wales, as well as doing nursery nursing in a boarding school for children of what used to be called British Colonials in Criccieth, North Wales. With her own three children now all grown up, she says she only started to take her writing more seriously about 12 years ago. Since then she has been coerced into getting all her pages of writing out of a carrier bag to turn into an anthology for her family.
"I have much to learn and write for fun," says Catherine. "But who knows the future?"

BEC WOODS

A first place in a short story competition for a Festival of Arts when she was eight set Bec on her way to wanting to be a writer. Along the way she's written the first draft of a novel in a month, completed a MA in Creative Writing with the Open University, and been a member of Ann's writing classes since they began in 2013. When she's not writing plays, poems or prose she enjoys reading and amongst her favourite writers are Kevin Barry, George Saunders, and Sarah Hall.

Bec's blog is https://atmywritingdesk.wordpress.com

Printed in Poland
by Amazon Fulfillment
Poland Sp. z o.o., Wrocław